Winter Honeymoon

Winter Honeymoon

············ *Stories* ············

Jacob M. Appel

Black
Lawrence
Press

Black Lawrence Press

www.blacklawrence.com

Executive Editor: Diane Goettel
Cover and book design: Amy Freels

Published 2020 by Black Lawrence Press.
Printed in the United States.

The following stories have previously appeared, sometimes in different form, in the following publications: "Winter Honeymoon" in *River Styx*; "The Appraisal" in *New York Stories*; "The Apprenticeship" in *North American Review*; "The Other Sister" in *Harpur Palate*; "Before the Storm" (as "Disaster Management") in *Washington Square*; "Iceberg Potential" in *Reservoir*; "Pay As You Go" in *Southern Humanities Review*; "After Valentino" in *Yemassee*; "Fallout" in *Colorado Review*.

For Rosalie & Kaely

Contents

· · · · · · · · · · · · · ·

Winter Honeymoon

During the final weeks of her husband's illness, Edith befriended the demented priest in the neighboring bed. Father Petrica was a cheerful, silver-haired man in his early sixties who spoke seven different languages with a thick Romanian accent. He'd fallen from a stepstool while changing a light bulb, fracturing ribs, vertebrae, both collarbones; later his brain swelled, unmooring his memories and inhibitions. Then kidney failure, skin infections, an amputated foot. The man stumbled from one setback to another, but courageously, like an imperial army in retreat. By the time Edith started reading aloud to him from Raymond Chandler novels, while Simon was away being MRI-ed and CT-scanned and surgically explored, the priest was innocently sharing tidbits collected over three decades behind the confessional.

One afternoon, Father Petrica proposed that they elope to Puerto Vallarta. "What do you say?" he asked. "We'll be just like Richard Burton and what's her name ..."

"Elizabeth Taylor," said Edith.

"That's right. Only she'll never hold a candle to you."

He clasped her left hand in both of his, and belted out *That's Amore*, surprisingly on key, but broke down coughing halfway through the second verse. Edith poured him a cup of water from a plastic bottle.

"I'm flattered," she said. "Really. But aren't you forgetting that you're a priest?"

"*I'm a priest?*" asked the priest. He grinned impishly, as though he had been the victim of a practical joke. "You are pulling me by the tail."

"*You're* a priest and *I'm* a married woman, as was Elizabeth Taylor when Richard Burton courted her." Edith spoke in the same firm-but-loving tone that she used to warn her second graders against stockpiling tree branches during recess. "I'm not even Catholic."

The priest digested this information. His large, genial features looked suddenly wistful. "So no Mexico?"

"I'm afraid not," said Edith.

She noticed the whiteboard sign beside Petrica's telephone: *GOOD MORNING. TODAY IS TUESDAY, JANUARY 18th*. It was actually Thursday, January 20th. Beyond Simon's empty bed, Edith could see jagged patches of ice on the Hudson River and New Jersey's snow-streaked cliffs. The priest swallowed the last of his water. He asked, "Do you regret anything?"

What a question! Who didn't have regrets at fifty-nine? But she wondered if her companion sensed something deeper, more personal, his insights growing clearer as his body withered. More likely, he was jabbing into the darkness like a fortuneteller. Or he wanted her confession: To hear her admit that she couldn't think of anything she *didn't* regret. Anything! Because she'd known from the outset that she'd married the wrong man—and now that she loved him anyway, he was mustering up the nerve to die on her.

"*I* have regrets," said Father Petrica. "I should have been Pope."

. . . . .

Five weeks later, she received the card from Kenneth, as she'd somehow known she would, and two days after that, Edith was driving up the New England coast toward Creve Coeur, Rhode Island. The morning was bright and cold. Through the naked trees flanking the highway, you could see swing sets and patios. She wondered which came first: the interstate or the houses. And had other families been uprooted to clear the route? More and more frequently, ever since her husband's diagnosis, Edith found herself searching for obliterated histories in familiar places. She'd telephoned the oldest alumna of the elementary school to learn what second grade had been like during World War I. She'd searched the archive at the New York Public Library for early images of their apartment building. Simon had been glad to see her busy. If her husband had owned one of those exposed homes, Edith reflected, he'd have put up a fence.

Kenneth had read Simon's obituary in the *Times*. The paper of record. The same paper that had once declined her wedding announcement. So this was a victory for Simon, she supposed, these two final columns above the fold. When you catalogued his achievements like that—all those honorary degrees, cardiology publications, celebrity patients—her late husband's life sounded so astonishingly impressive. Of course, someday Kenneth's death would make front pages across the country. Which was a truly morbid thing to be thinking. Yet here she was thinking it.

Edith stopped at the new welcome center just across the Connecticut border. A busload of Asian tourists had pulled in ahead of her, so she thumbed through the free brochures while she waited for the ladies' room. Inevitably, there was a flyer for Little Europa: "See the great cities of the world without leaving Rhode Island." The photo showed St. Mark's Basilica and the Doge's Palace constructed from thimbles, foreign coins and laminated candy bar wrappers. Edith had visited the real Venice twice, accompanying Simon to medical conferences, but she'd seen

Kenneth's replicas only on postcards at the Museum of Modern Art. She'd purchased the complete set.

Since her parents had passed on, she'd returned to Creve Coeur just once. Yet she had little trouble finding Kenneth's quirky masterpiece, following roadside cutouts of the Arc de Triomphe to what had once been known as Tanner's Hill, the seat of a thriving, nineteenth century trade in leather goods. During Edith's girlhood, the neighborhood—like the much of the city—had incrementally depopulated. What had been a whaling hub, and then the continent's ladies' boot manufacturing capital, became the moribund ghost city that her father had dubbed: "New Haven without a college." But now Kenneth's odd creations drew tens of thousands of visitors.

From the steep, tortuous driveway, climbing between vacant, red-brick warehouses, you could make out a few landmarks above the distant evergreen hedge: the famed soup-can tower of Pisa, the domes of the Kremlin, turrets that might belong to Aswan or Istanbul. Even on a chilly weekday afternoon, the parking lot was packed. Edith followed a slate path around a miniature Taj Mahal and past a bustling gift shop to a one-story, wood-frame office that smelled artificially of pine. Beside the plastered-in fireplace, on a wicker rocking chair, dozed the fattest Siamese cat that Edith had ever encountered. Framed posters for *It's A Wonderful Life* and *The Wizard of Oz* hung over the mantle. The pudgy girl behind the counter was speaking on the phone, what sounded like an argument with her boyfriend over the cost of new muffler. She pressed the receiver against her shoulder and looked up at Edith impatiently.

"I'm hoping to see Mr. Wondra," said Edith.

"Do you have an appointment?"

"Not exactly," said Edith. "But—" But what? But I'm the woman who didn't marry him thirty-five years ago, so he'll want to see me?

She didn't even know whether Kenneth had a wife, a family. "We're old friends. We went to grade school together."

"Mr. Wondra's not here today," said the girl. "He works at home."

"I drove all the way from New York. Can you call him?"

The girl didn't acknowledge the request overtly. She told her boyfriend she'd phone him back and then asked for Edith's name. Edith gently shook the cat from the chair and settled down to wait, wondering how she'd ever become so pushy.

· · · · ·

Happiness requires flexibility, Edith knew. Not lowered expectations, but malleable ones. Intransigence is what hardens arteries and souls.

The last time she'd seen Kenneth, other than on a PBS documentary, Richard Nixon had been President. Her parents had still been alive. Sissy Collins, a girl in her freshman dormitory at Barnard, had just been killed in a skiing mishap—and, at the time, *that* had seemed like the end of the world. Oh, Sissy Collins! Who wrote a mildly salacious weekly column for the *Barnard Bulletin* and had dreamed of becoming the next Hedda Hopper. When did Edith ever think about her now? But during that long-lost weekend in early December, after Kenneth had hitchhiked down from Creve Coeur on the back of a truck hauling Christmas trees, Sissy's death had crept into every conversation as a frigid draught slinks around panes of glass. Edith hadn't known anyone her own age who'd died before. Not well. Her classmate's accident was her first warning that life, for all its pleasures, was inherently unreasonable.

She'd taken Kenneth to the cozy Greek pastry shop across from the Episcopal Cathedral, where the one-eyed proprietor served tiny glasses of mint liqueur alongside the coffee, and an obese Romanian woman offered to interpret the grinds for two dollars. Kenneth ducked outside while Edith wavered between the amygdalopita and the baklava, and he returned with a red beauty rose from the corner florist. She doubted he'd actually paid for the flower—but that was a pointless conversation. She peeled the thorns off the stem and watched the restaurant reflected through the long salon mirror. How wondrous Kenneth looked with his enormous sculptor's hands and adorably asymmetrical ears! She felt like a mason about to carve into stone.

"Why not?" he asked—picking up a thread of their earlier conversation. "Look at it objectively, Edie. You can learn more hanging out in Europe for one day than in four years of college."

Edith trailed her fork aimlessly over the crust of the baklava. "They don't give you a diploma for hanging out in Europe."

"What's that supposed to mean?" snapped Kenneth.

Kenneth had put off college. He'd tossed his draft card over the railing of the Narragansett ferry. He was living rent-free above his father's dental office, in a semi-furnished room, selling hand-whittled wax and soap sculptures at the farmers' market for spending money. Now his plan was to slum across Europe, crashing with fellow "folk artists." He rolled a cigarette and blew a perfect loop of smoke.

"Look, I've met someone," said Edith—surprising herself. "Someone else."

"You've got to be kidding me."

Kenneth glared at her as though she'd harpooned him. Then he slammed his fist into the wooden tabletop, shaking the porcelain sugar bowl and the creamer.

"Please don't get angry," begged Edith.

"What do you want me to do? Dance in the fucking streets?"

She glanced at the neighboring tables, fearful that she was

provoking a scene. But the couples surrounding them—graduate students and their hangers-on, in various states of self-absorption and dishevelment—hardly took notice. "What I want," said Edith, "is for you to go to college . . . or get a job . . . or join the war protestors, for heaven's sake. Do you know how it feels when I tell people my boyfriend carves candles for a living?"

"Let me guess. Lover-boy is President of General Motors."

The truth was she'd only gone out with Simon three times. He was a medical student at Cornell, a nephew of a physics professor she typed letters for, and on their first date he'd entertained her with a list of amusing things that doctors had allegedly written on hospital charts: "The patient has no previous history of suicides"; "Examination of genitalia revealed that he is circus sized"; " A full pelvic exam will be done later on the floor." These were probably apocryphal—like the errors school children purportedly made on standardized exams—but they were funny nonetheless.

"Please don't make a big deal of this," she pleaded, retreating. "I don't know if it's anything. I don't even know if I like him."

"You *don't* like him," said Kenneth. "You just *think* you like him."

"That's not fair," said Edith.

"I know you better than you do, Edie Moss." Kenneth grinned bitterly. "You'll probably marry Lover-boy just to spite me."

They'd walked back to her dormitory in silence, across the gray shadows of the Columbia campus, and then they'd argued bitterly until nearly dawn—so bitterly, that on his way through the foyer, Kenneth piled all of her footwear into a paper shopping bag and stormed out of the building. He'd even included her bath slippers and her ice skates.

He sent them back to her, two weeks later, by express mail. The package arrived the same afternoon that she announced her engagement to Simon.

. . . . .

Now what struck Edith first was how right Kenneth looked. How calm. As though sixty had always been his internal age, and his body had finally caught up. He was wearing a plaid shirt under his denim jacket and a knitted orange cap; his full auburn beard had gone silver at the fringes like the mane of an aging lion. But he was as tall and imposing as ever, not prematurely diminished as Simon had become. She'd nearly forgotten that Kenneth had to duck under low entryways.

He pulled the door shut behind him, jangling a tiny bell.

"Edie," he said. "Edie Moss."

"Edie Kindler," she said reflexively—regretting the words as she spoke them.

"Obviously," agreed Kenneth. "Edie Kindler."

He walked to the counter and deposited a stack of letters in front of the pudgy girl. "I'm going to give Mrs. Kindler a guided tour. Can you phone Becky and let her know I won't be back until late?" Then he turned toward Edith and explained, although explanation was unnecessary: "My niece is staying with me. Gloria's step-daughter. She's taking a year off before art school." He reached forward, as the he might stroke her hair, but it was only to retrieve a scarf from the hook above the rocker. "If I'd known you were coming..."

What? Edith wondered. *What would you have done if you'd known I was coming?* Probably nothing different. And how did little "Morning Glory" Wondra ever end up with a college-age girl of her own? The idea of other women having children left a vinegary taste in Edith's mouth.

"Let's go see the sights," suggested Kenneth. "Just don't blow my cover."

"You mean you won't get recognized?"

"I sure hope not. There's a reason my picture's not on the brochures."

He held the door open for her and followed her into the nipping chill. They walked side by side up the slate path, like a married couple. Between the parapets of Machu Picchu. Beyond Stonehenge and Tintern Abbey and Córdoba with its linoleum bridges and corrugated aluminum mosque. "The fountains are fully functional," observed Kenneth, "but we shut them off for the winter." He gently took hold of her elbow, to steer her through a vine-wrapped arbor, and did not let go. She stole a glimpse of his left hand. There were no rings.

"I can't begin to express how impressive this all is," said Edith.

"Thank you," answered Kenneth. Not a hint of false modesty, just the candor of a man confident enough to accept a compliment. "It took a while, but I'm glad I did it."

"I am too," said Edith.

He glanced at her inquisitively. "Let's avoid Italy and take the back stairs up to the mountains," he proposed.

Kenneth unlocked a wrought iron gate and they climbed a steep concrete staircase that rose along the perimeter of the exhibits. A waterproof emerald canopy sheltered the path. You could hear the sightseers on the other side of the mesh, but you couldn't see them. As the trail narrowed, the two of them were forced to walk single file. Through a minefield of folded sawhorses, coiled garden hoses, buckets of grout stacked pyramidally like acrobats. It reminded Edith of the time Simon had arranged a heart transplant for the chief keeper at the Bronx Zoo, and they'd received a private, off-hours tour. "There's this guy in Japan, trained as an industrial welder, who's doing the same thing inside suitcases," said Kenneth. "It's called Portable Cities. You open your valise and out jumps Angkor Wat or the Great Wall of China."

"Like a pop-up book," said Edith.

At the top landing, Kenneth unlocked a second gate. They stood opposite two snow-covered peaks. "That's the Matterhorn. This here's Mount Blanc. Straight out of a Shelley poem. The snow is shaved fiberglass from indoor swimming pools," said Kenneth. "I bet you never thought you'd see the Alps and the Andes in the same afternoon."

Edith hadn't read a Romantic poem since Barnard. To her, Mount Blanc meant pens. "This is like being on a honeymoon," she said. "A magical honeymoon."

At that moment, a mousy, henna-haired woman approached them and asked if Kenneth would mind photographing her in front of the Riffelsee. For her nephew in Switzerland. "When I was in Vegas," she said, "I had my picture taken outside the Luxor and sent it to my nephew in Cairo. My other nephew." The woman was about Edith's age and apparently travelling alone. Kenneth snapped a photo. And then a second *to be certain*. He returned the camera to the mousy woman and urged her to keep warm.

"That's my favorite part," said Kenneth. "She'll see my picture someday and she'll realize who I was. I tell you, Edie, it's a strange world."

Something in Kenneth's tone suggested intimacy, an acknowledgement that they were more than merely two old friends sharing a visit. Edith said nothing.

"Are you okay?" he asked.

She nodded. "I was just thinking of Sissy Collins."

Kenneth smiled sympathetically, but without recognition.

"The girl in my dorm who was killed in the skiing accident. *From Barnard*. Do you still remember that?"

"Maybe. Vaguely," said Kenneth. "This probably goes without saying, but I'm really sorry about Simon. Sincerely, I am."

"Of course, you are."

"I never thought I'd say that," added Kenneth. "But I am."

. . . . .

The rabbi at the cemetery had asked her about Simon's life. They weren't at all religious, but they owned plots in a Jewish memorial park, the third generation of Kindlers to be eternally ensconced in suburban New Jersey, so twenty minutes of Rabbi Gershon's graveside blather were included with the casket and the hearse. The girl must have been fresh out of the seminary. She was so nervous, so stiff. Edith felt genuinely sorry for her. But even that couldn't prevent her from answering the girl's prescribed questions with a dash of astringent humor.

"What made Dr. Kindler a righteous soul?" the rabbi asked.

"I suppose *I* did," Edith answered, "on good days."

This obviously wasn't what the young rabbi had meant. "Let me ask that a different way. What was it about Dr. Kindler that made you love him?"

Edith almost blurted out: *Because he was good in the sack.* Which was true, but not the reason she loved him. Nor was it his patience, his decency, his ability to keep calm under pressure. Not even his dry wit, how he playfully included a slice of pastrami among the medical students' pathology samples in order to keep them on their toes. These were the qualities that made her *like* Simon. But loving was something different. Maybe what it came down to was how vulnerable he'd looked lying there in bed beside her each night—the way, at the hospital, he could supervise two dozen residents, and perform fifty angioplasties a week, and deliver off-the-cuff lectures before audiences of three hundred specialists, but in bed, when he shut his eyes and sank into the pillows, he was as powerless and as exposed as a blind baby kitten. Maybe that was also why she loved her second graders. Because she could protect them—at least for the briefest interval. Was this what really held together their marriage? The knowledge that if not for her vigilance, a late-night prowler might have crushed Simon's skull with a rolling pin. Quite possibly. But this was not the sort of soul-baring insight one offered a rabbi before a funeral.

"Can I ask you something?" asked Edith.

"Please," said the rabbi. "Ask anything."

"Don't you think it's peculiar that people live entirely secular lives and still get buried in religiously segregated cemeteries?"

. . . . .

"I thought about asking her whether it was to help God sort the saved from the damned," Edith mused, "but I was already giving her such a hard time."

They were arm-in-arm again. Somewhere in Scandinavia.

"Death is an odd business," Kenneth answered. "Death and love. The great cosmic mysteries."

"Don't forget art," said Edith. "Surely that must be a cosmic mystery."

"Art? Maybe for Vermeer. What I do is a lot more like shoveling snow."

Edith laughed at that. Because she knew he wasn't joking. Because living in Manhattan, she'd forgotten all about shoveling snow. Strolling with Kenneth made her feel carefree for the first time since Simon's diagnosis, maybe even long before that. As though she were on vacation in *fin-de-siècle* Paris.

"Nobody believes me when I tell them that," he said.

"I believe you."

They'd reached the frontiers of the park—where a man-made stream flowed miraculously out of the rockface. It was the same channel that fed the Rhine and the Danube and the Volga. The water descended through tiered pools, in which moorhens and mergansers and a solitary Canada goose sunned themselves. From the far bank, a raggedy squirrel eyed Edith suspiciously. Kenneth pointed out a swan nesting behind a concrete dam. If Kenneth had tried to kiss her, she would have let him. Instead, he said, "You haven't asked me why I've built this. *Everyone* asks me that."

The notion swept Edith's mind that he'd created this monument entirely for her. As a shrine to lost love. "Okay. Why did you build it?" she asked coyly.

"I have no clue. None at all," Kenneth answered. "I used to tell people that it was the poor man's grand tour. A way for working class stiffs to experience all the sights they'd never see in person. But that was just Marxist bullshit. It sounded good. Between you, me and the wind, Edie Kindler, I've devoted my entire life to this project and I don't have the foggiest idea of why. Sounds pretty far-fetched, doesn't it?"

"But you're happy?"

They started walking again. "Yes, I *am* happy. Are you? I mean, other than..."

"Other than *that*, Mrs. Lincoln," said Edith, "how did you enjoy the play?"

The breeze picked up. She placed her hand in the pocket of his jacket, like she'd done when they went steady in high school; he didn't object. Inside, her fingers found a workman's pencil and a small polished stone.

"I'm on family leave this semester. There are days when I miss the children even more than I miss Simon. They'll be doing their winter dioramas right about now." Edith's eyes grew moist: a flood of present sorrow and cold air and long-sought relief. "Can we see Paris?" she asked impulsively. But the question held more weight than she'd intended, as though she'd actually proposed a trip to another continent.

"Do you *really* want to see Paris?" Kenneth sounded disappointed.

"Is that all right?"

"Paris will be crawling with teenage couples and French Canadians on their second honeymoons. How about Mexico? You'll like it much more."

Something in Kenneth's tone irked her. That he would still try to reshape her, even now. Soon the roof combs of the Mayan temples rose into view, but she had little desire to see them.

"A man once asked me to run off to Mexico with him," she said.

"I'm not the slightest bit surprised," said Kenneth. "You're a beautiful woman. I imagine you've had your share of offers over the years."

Edith sensed he'd retreated—maybe taking a cue. In his compliment hung a forced indifference that diminished their own lost romance.

"A few," she said. "Not as many as you think."

The truth was there had only been one.

· · · · ·

The first postcard had been waiting for her after her honeymoon. They'd spent the week in Cape May, New Jersey, because Simon couldn't afford to get away for longer. To her husband, it was so cut-and-dried: Why spent six days in Hawaii when someday they could spent six weeks there? And he'd kept his promise. For their thirtieth anniversary, he'd arranged a two month visiting professorship in Honolulu. But returning home to Kenneth's memento from Lisbon left Edith enraged—at both the man she'd married and at the man she hadn't. The card showed an interior view of the cloisters at the Jerónimos Monastery, the sort of free postcard that advertised a youth hostel across the front. Next came a triangular card from the Basque Country. Later more cards from Brittany, Liege, Hamburg. For a while, she'd feared Kenneth was traveling solely for the purpose of sending her mail. But the notes were brief, innocuous. Even the aerograms from Warsaw and Gdansk were so extravagantly bland that they must have confounded the Polish censors. Simon took no interest in these notes; he was neither jealous nor intrusive. At first, Edith thought them threatening. But after the first six months or so, she found herself taking an odd comfort in their consistency. What did she have to be afraid of? She was married, wasn't she? That ought to be armor enough.

But then Kenneth returned to Rhode Island. He sent her a kind note when her father died, a longer letter when her mother passed on. With the letter, he included a clipping from the *Creve Coeur Courant* about his exhibit, "Little London and Petit Paris." This was during one of the frostiest patches in Edith's marriage, when Simon traveled constantly, and her body started telling her what the endocrinologists would later confirm—that she would never have her own children. So when Kenneth phoned one Sunday afternoon while Simon was in Little Rock, addressing the annual convention of the Arkansas Hypertension Association, it was Edith who suggested the rendezvous. Coffee, she'd said. A chance to catch up. Whether she'd intended more, she wasn't certain. But she never mentioned her plans to Simon.

They'd chosen the following Saturday. That was after her parent-teacher conferences were done, before Kenneth's impending two-month trip to South America. A crisp, sunny afternoon in late October. Simon would be 30,000 feet over the Rust Belt on his way to a weekend conference at the Mayo Clinic, while Edith cruised up the New England coast in her husband's sporty new Saab, feeling as though she were driving a stolen vehicle. She'd seen Simon to the door that morning, reminded him to request his frequent flyer miles. A cop in Branford, Connecticut, pulled her over for passing illegally on the right—but let her escape *just his once* with a warning. She turned onto High Street, across from the Clam & Oyster, at twenty minutes to twelve.

She'd met Kenneth at the Clam & Oyster a thousand times before. It was a cozy, dimly-lit pub that sold coffee and cold sandwiches on weekend afternoons. But no shellfish. The proprietor's father had served six years in the navy. On shore leave in Liverpool, he'd come across a bar with the same name, and brought it back with him. "And that joint didn't serve seafood either," the old salt liked to say. "Guy who owned the place was named Clam—Bert Clam—and he made up Oyster for a partner." Edith peered through the plate glass. They'd put in new booths along the far wall, and broad wooden ceiling fans, but the menu hadn't changed. Nor had the woman behind the counter. She'd been a few years ahead of Edith at Chafee High School. Now she must have been close to forty. While Edith had gone off to college in New York City and married Simon, this girl—Carol or Cheryl—had stayed right where she was.

The restaurant was nearly empty. The proprietor, his formerly salt-and-pepper hair dyed jet-black, wandered from vacant booth to vacant both, lighting candles. A Rheingold clock hung above the bar, perpetually frozen at ten past two.

The counter girl offered Edith a table, but she said no. Somehow, the thought of sitting alone made her feel claustrophobic—as though she might order a soft drink and then be trapped at her perch for hours. She preferred the sidewalk, where she could window-shop and peruse the flyers stapled to the telephone poles. *Discount acupuncture. Discount piano lessons. A rally to free Rhode Island's political prisoners.* Also many rusted staples attached to nothing, a reminder of life's missed opportunities. Gulls circled overhead. A taxicab honked for a late fare. The stench of the ocean rose from the Portuguese fish market. Soon, Edith's fingers grew cold and she decided to wait for Kenneth inside the car.

He arrived at exactly twelve o'clock and peered for her through the Clam & Oyster's front window, then enjoyed a cigarette on the sidewalk. Edith waved from the far side of the narrow street—a spontaneous impulse—but quickly realized that he couldn't see her through the Saab's tinted glass. And this relieved her, in some inexplicable way, knowing that she hadn't yet committed herself. What she didn't do next was to get out of the vehicle and announce her presence. Instead, she waited and watched. After a second smoke, Kenneth went into the restaurant. He chatted briefly with the counter girl, probably asking after Edith, and took a table by the juke box.

Kenneth waited another three hours. Chain smoking, reading. Edith could just make out the word BOLIVIA printed across the front of his book. When the happy hour crowd straggled in, he ordered a cup of coffee and a sandwich. And then he departed. She caught the look on his face as he crossed back up the block toward the bus stop. He did not appear heartbroken, merely displeased. Like a man served the wrong meal in a restaurant.

Edith sobbed all the way home. On the outskirts of the city, she turned on the radio news—suddenly, irrationally convinced that Simon's plane had crashed into an Iowa cornfield, and that she had been left all alone.

After that, there were no more postcards from Kenneth. No more phone calls. Nothing. And then one day, one year, she was deeply in love with her husband, and the thought that Kenneth might call sent a nervous chill across her flesh.

· · · · ·

"He died," Edith said sharply. "The friend who invited me to Puerto Vallarta died. A few days before Simon."

"Puerto Vallarta is a stunning city," Kenneth answered. "Let me show you."

He placed his arm gently on her back and led her forward. She felt a surge of unreasonable anger toward him. She considered asking why he hadn't come searching for her that day—why he hadn't phoned her in New York City? She might have skidded off the highway and been dead in a ditch! But why go into that now?

"My friend fell off a goddam ladder," said Edith. "Sixty-two years old."

"You've had a hard run of it," Kenneth said. "You know, Edie, I've thought about you many times over the years. Don't think I haven't."

"I don't know what to think," she said.

Her tone was unkind, and he said no more.

They walked a good distance farther in complete silence. Eventually, they arrived at a small coastal village shielded by coconut palms. The trees were fashioned from men's pocket combs, the fruit from hacky-sacks and stuffed baby booties. Puerto Vallarta. Kenneth's hallmark of obsessive care was apparent in the individual, hand-wrought planks along the boardwalk, and the tiny cocktail olives in the sunset-bar drinks, and the fine exterior stairs circling the spires of Our Lady of Guadeloupe. A miniature *Love Boat* sat at anchor in the harbor. Kenneth used a broken stick to indicate the colonial-style villa on Gringo Gulch, Casa Kimberley, where Richard Burton had seduced Elizabeth Taylor while she was still married to Eddie Fisher. Edith felt like a tourist and was seized with a desire to return home.

She glanced at her watch. "I'd best get going soon," she said. "Otherwise, I'll get caught in traffic."

He nodded. "Already?"

"Thank you for the tour," Edith said.

That sounded so formal. But she didn't know what else to say. The regrets and hopes she had planned to share with Kenneth, this parallel world avoided for half a lifetime and then suddenly craved, had just as suddenly crumbled—like an ancient relic preserved for centuries that falls to dust upon the first human touch. She was already thinking about her second graders, about how Simon would not sleep next to her that night, about how she might take over his garden in the coming spring, stoically tending his daylilies and his peonies. She was already thinking about the long ride home.

Kenneth walked her to the parking lot through the main gate and they hugged briefly. Like dear old friends. If he'd squeezed her longer, she might have held on, in spite of everything. But he didn't. Neither of them did.

The Appraisal

· ·

"Sixty-three," said Abbie. "Half a life."

She stood at the open window and gazed through the bars. Outside, the city pulsed in its usual frenzy. A street merchant had spread his wares on the sidewalk in front of the school—books, records, baseball memorabilia. Across Riverside Drive, a dark-skinned nanny wheeled two light-skinned babies in a stroller. Farther down the block, an elderly Chinese couple was shaking the branches of the ginko trees. They did this every June, collecting bucketfuls of the soft, stinking fruit. Abbie wondered what they did with the fruit, but she'd never gotten around to asking.

"They're making progress every day," said Bert. "All sorts of advances."

Abbie turned to face him. "It's funny. I can remember when anything past sixty seemed absolutely ancient." She surveyed the bare classroom. In one corner stood the boxes of picture books and art supplies that belonged to St. Mary's. Two smaller cartons, marked PERSONAL, would go home with her. "Did you know that when my grandmother turned eighty, she received a framed certificate from President Truman?"

"You can fight this," said Bert. "Don't croak on one doctor's opinion."

"To what end? To die like Leonard?" asked Abbie. "I won't go through that."

She'd married Leonard shortly after Bert had divorced her. (Sometimes she quipped she'd lost one husband to another man, the other to another world.) Leonard's final months in the chronic care facility—she called it the *gulag*—had been wretched. He'd suffered a series of small strokes. Each carried off a piece of him, as water smooths sand. Finally, nothing remained but a cask of withered flesh.

"Is there anything I can say?" asked Bert. He was sitting on her desk, his short legs dangling over the side. Much of his hair was long gone. The orange tufts at the corners of his scalp resembled giant earmuffs. "What haven't I thought of?"

"I asked *you* that, once," answered Abbie. "Remember?" That had been the morning he'd revealed his relationship with Wesley, an episode now almost inaccessibly remote. She crossed the room and settled beside him on the desktop. For the first time in thirty years, she took his hand in hers. "It's too late to say anything," she said. "I know what death's about. And I'm not afraid of it, not terribly. But to end up alone in a sterile white room with a handful of meager possessions—*that* scares the living shit out of me."

Bert nodded, polishing his forehead with his stubby fingers.

"I've thought everything through," continued Abbie. "Having a tumor in your lung makes your mind work overtime." She liked to imagine the growth as a walnut-sized kernel, solid but delicate like the heart of a songbird. That, of course, had been months ago— before the diagnosis, before the cancer slithered into her bones. "I haven't led the life I wanted," Abbie said.

"You've taught all these children."

"But I didn't change them. Not the way some teachers do." For years she'd labored at it, but teaching wasn't her gift. Her wit confused the children. Eventually, she'd given up trying. "It was a waste," she said. "I want my death to have meaning."

"To raise awareness," agreed Bert.

Abbie squeezed his hand. "In a way. I'm going to set myself on fire."

Bert said nothing, at first. Abbie stared down at her toes, then across the room at the globe and the filing cabinet. Under the American flag, the oscillating fan whirred with silent grace.

"To protest the war," Abbie explained. "Like during Vietnam."

"You're serious?"

"Dead serious," she answered. "That's why I called you."

"You can't do this," said Bert.

"I can do this. I *will* do this. And I need your help."

·····

The idea had come to Abbie at the beauty salon.

Usually, she had her hair done around the corner. Her stylist, Vin, was a no-nonsense gay kid from the streets of Baltimore. He worked quickly. He had thick, steady hands you could trust not to lop your ears off. Both of his grandfathers had been barbers back in Sicily. She'd always thought his shop cozy, a blend of Old Neighborhood and Old World, but now, with the claw of death reaching for her across the horizon, it struck her as insufferably drab. *So much* of her past, her present, suddenly seemed insufferably drab—as though she'd lived, unknowingly, to the wattage of a low-energy bulb. Maybe that was why, on the morning after her diagnosis, Abbie walked rapidly past Vin's window and crossed Amsterdam Avenue to the hip, glitzy salon that had replaced the Filipino laundromat. She'd craved change. She wanted to spend money frivolously.

All of the furniture in the new salon was black and angular. The women waiting ahead of her were half her age, probably half her weight. Abbie sat down. She pulled *The Forsyte Saga* from her canvas bag. The book seemed unreasonably long. Was it worth the investment? It might be the last book she'd ever read. The girl in the next chair, a bleached blonde with an eyebrow ring, was reading *Beyond the Perfect Orgasm*. Maybe that was a preferable choice. Or possibly Proust. Unable to concentrate, Abbie folded shut her novel. A conversation between two of the stylists caught her attention, though several seconds elapsed as she laced together its threads.

"But would you do it?" asked the stylist nearest the window. She was a small, sharp-featured young woman. She reminded Abbie of an angry pigeon. "I mean if there were no personal consequences. If you could walk away scot-free."

"Fuck, Summer," said her male coworker. He was tall and emaciated—what Abbie called *concentration camp chic*. His voice rolled in waves. "Where do you think up these questions?"

"They just come to me," said Summer.

Summer snipped a few final strands from the bangs of a statuesque brunette, cutting more empty space than hair. Her work struck Abbie as impersonal. It was like getting trimmed by a topiary gardener.

"Think about all the suffering he's caused," Summer persisted. "You would have killed Hitler, wouldn't you?"

"Jesus Christ," said her co-worker. "I don't know."

It suddenly registered with Abbie: These kids were talking about assassinating the President. Abstractly, of course. But nonetheless a sorry statement about the plight of the world, about the incompetent lunatics she would no longer live to see destroy it. This was the second time she'd overheard strangers discussing the President's death. The previous week, she'd had dinner with a retired colleague. The couple at the next table, clearly on a first date, were debating the appropriate response to learning that the

madman in the Oval Office had been shot. He'd said glee. She'd
insisted upon tempered relief. Halfway through the meal, they were
kissing. Meanwhile, Abbie's companion lamented a world gone to
hell in a hand basket. "When JFK died," he'd said, "I lost a brother."

When Kennedy was shot, Abbie had been younger than the
stylist.

"I'd do it too," said Summer, decisively. "I really would."

Her coworker signaled for the next woman in line. "So it's
settled," he said.

The brunette rose from Summer's chair. She was closer to
Abbie's age than the stylist's, strikingly attractive, though the
skin of her face was a bit too tight. "I don't think you should kill
anybody," she interjected. "Ever." Her voice held a deep sadness.
"If you're upset with things—and there's certainly enough to be
upset about—you should put yourself on the line. Like Gandhi or
Martin Luther King."

"I guess so," agreed Summer.

The brunette stepped around Summer. Abbie assumed her
place in the chair. When the woman had paid and departed, the
male stylist said, "Way to upset the customers."

"Screw you," said Summer. "I'm still right." She scooped up Abbie's
hair in her bony white hand. "What are we going to do today?"

"Not much," said Abbie. "I want to look like Grace Kelly."

The stylist smiled blankly. Abbie felt old and useless.

"Just a joke," she said. "Whatever you sense works best."

Already, though, she was thinking about putting herself on the
line. She'd never done anything *particularly* political before, but
the need had never seemed so great. Besides, it would help make
up for frittering her life away. That, after all, was what she'd done.
She'd never opened up that catering company, never gone back
for her doctorate. Instead, she'd passed her days keeping things

in their place. (And there'd been so many minor crises, dripping knapsacks, bruised elbows, valises left on airplanes . . .) And now Leonard was dead. Her parents were dead. Her son, Norman, was as good as dead—she hadn't spoken to him in a decade. (The boy hadn't even come to his father's funeral.) For years it had torn her apart, had nearly torn her marriage apart. She'd tried visiting him once, in prison, when he served time for passing bad checks. He'd have none of it. Another of her many failures. Thinking about Norman made Abbie truly miserable, so she no longer did.

Summer massaged shampoo into her scalp. "Do you think you'd like some color? Maybe a hint of vermilion?"

"Yes," said Abbie, indifferently. "Whatever."

She was recollecting the first time she'd seen Leonard teach. He'd been a bioethics professor at Columbia. "Do you know what this is?" he asked, holding up a straggly yard of rope. He paced the lecture hall effervescently, sweat beading at his temples. "Not any old string," he declaimed. "Not your run-of-the-mill, butcher's block string. No, no, Nanette! This is my *lucky* piece of string." Here Leonard had paused, leaning forward over his lectern. The veins bulged above his temples. A thin drop of perspiration glistened at the end of his nose. "If you intentionally destroy my lucky piece of string," he demanded, "to how much compensation am I entitled?" And then he'd asked about human life: What was it worth? How was "Grandma"—unemployable, of limited social use—any more valuable than his lucky piece of string? Abbie's first husband, Bert, was an appraiser of artwork and collectibles. But Leonard—Leonard had been an appraiser of lives.

"Maybe you should kill yourself," said Abbie.

The stylist was still kneading Abbie's head. "What, honey?"

"Self-immolation. Don't kill the President. Kill yourself in protest."

As she said the words, they struck Abbie as surprisingly compelling. Later—when she shared her plans with Bert—she would realize how much easier it was to make the decision than to explain it. She'd compared it to coming up with the idea for a bedtime story. "It wasn't there. And then it was." Eventually, if you told yourself the story enough times, as she would do over the coming weeks, its every thread seemed inevitable. These reflections, of course, would come later. Sitting in the salon chair, her hair matted in lather, all Abbie knew was that she'd found a plausible alternative to a death of quiet desperation. The previous night, she'd counted barbiturates in preparation for a private end. Now a public departure rose before her, a grand gesture. That was the sort of hook you could hang your life on.

Abbie drew her head up. Soapy water trickled down her back.

"What the hell?" exclaimed Summer.

Abbie rummaged in her purse. She closed the girl's hand around three crisp twenty dollar bills.

"Fuck, honey," shouted Summer. "What's wrong?"

"I'm dying," Abbie answered, smiling.

She brushed past the dumbstruck stylist and hurried outside. It was a bright, promising afternoon. The sidewalks were crowded. Several pedestrians glanced uncomfortably at Abbie. Most ignored her. Abbie didn't care. She walked home briskly, trailing water and suds up Ninety-First Street.

. . . . .

Bert's encounter with his ex-wife left him jittery. When he'd driven down to meet Abigail at St. Mary's, forty miles south of Chatham Valley, he'd initially hoped to knock off other errands. A college friend had recently acquired an étagère at a rummage sale. The man thought it might be valuable and had asked Bert to take a look. Also, Bert wanted to buy fresh oysters for Wes. And then there was the forgery case in which he was to be an expert witness, one of the perks of semi-retirement. For weeks, the lawyers had been on his back about dropping off the affidavits. Before visiting Abigail, Bert had planned to wipe clean his to-be-done list. Afterwards, of course, he'd been useless.

He found Wes out in the yard, digging a trench around his vegetable garden. This was the latest salvo in his futile war against woodchucks.

"You're home early," said Wes.

Bert dabbed his brow with his handkerchief. "What's that old Chinese curse? May you live in interesting times."

"That bad, eh?"

"Worse."

Bert recounted the morning's trauma. Wes continued to dig. He'd slung his t-shirt over a wooden fencepost, baring the lean muscle of his chest. At seventy, Wesley Rockford was still "the straightest gay man in the lower forty-eight." Sport fisherman. Hockey fan. One-time petrochemical engineer. (He claimed that in his native Alaska, some gay men were even straighter.) Wes had lost three fingers in a childhood hunting accident, leaving a right hand like a vintage baseball mitt. When he shoveled, he used only his left arm.

"It wasn't just the cancer," said Bert. "Or the suicide plan. It was all of it together. You had to see her there in that empty classroom—Those stacks of tiny chairs—Good God! She looked so . . ."

"Diminished?"

"Yeah," said Bert. "Diminished."

He sat down on the grass, using his jacket as a pillow. That portion of the lawn had been newly mowed. Later, Wes would rake up the clumps of fresh chaff.

"Abigail's mother was also a smoker," added Bert—to no particular purpose. "She also quit too late."

Wes kicked a clod of dirt off his shovel. He picked up a small stone and lobbed it into the rhododendron hedge. "Are you asking for advice?"

Bert shrugged. "Who knows? It hasn't sunk in yet."

"I imagine not."

"It's something Buddhist monks do." Bert wiped a tear from his eye. "Her sense of humor hasn't changed though—for better or for worse. She said that even a chef as bad as I am can rustle up Abigail Richmond flambé."

"I never thought of your ex as so political," said Wes.

"That's just it. She isn't. Not actively."

"Desperate measures for desperate times, eh?"

"Yeah," said Bert. "Something like that."

Wes tossed his shovel into a mound of red earth. He settled onto the grass, resting the back of his neck against Bert's abdomen. They lay in silence. Wes's head rose and fell with Bert's breath. Bert knew they were sharing the same thought: How grateful they were that they were together—*that Bert had left Abigail.* Cleaning the attic the previous spring, Bert had discovered the letters he'd written to Wes in Alaska. Their urgency stunned him. Certainly, he'd never loved Abigail so intensely.

He ran a hand through Wes's thick gray hair. "I owe it to her," he said.

"To help her or to stop her?"

"Exactly," said Bert. A bank of cotton clouds rolled across the sky. Another cloud drift hunkered at the horizon. Darker clouds, the color of steel wool. As a child, he'd had a knack for finding secrets in clouds—rabbits, owls, dragons. In Pelican Bay, Florida. A long time ago.

"Let's go inside," he said. "Before it rains."

.....

This was the first year of Bert's semi-retirement. Their friends had warned him against this arrangement. When you're ready, they said, go whole hog. Half-retired was like partially pregnant, somewhat unique. Often, it meant premature idleness. Time would weigh heavily upon him. The reality—in his case—had been decidedly the opposite. He'd had too many offers, not enough hours in the day. He still undertook special projects for his former employer, the city's leading auction house. Insurance companies offered him lucrative consulting fees. A prominent niche publisher wanted him to lend his name and expertise to a line of coffee table books. Bert didn't delude himself. He wasn't a household name. But by hook and by crook, he'd risen to the top of his field. Not shabby for the self-taught son of a Welsh pawnbroker.

"Maybe I feel guilty," he told Wes. "My life worked out. Hers didn't."

They were walking up Broadway toward Abigail's building. They were late. Parking had taken forever.

"Count no man happy until he dies," quoted Wes.

"Meaning?"

"It's Oedipus. Greek for 'Don't jinx us.'"

Bert grinned. He pressed Abigail's buzzer. Her building didn't have an elevator, so they walked up the six narrow flights of stairs.

Abigail greeted them at the door. She kissed Bert's cheek, shook Wes's hand. "Catch your breath," she said.

"I forgot how steep those stairs are," said Bert, coughing.

She laughed. "The cost of high ceilings."

The flat was just as Bert remembered. Tasteful, a tad stuffy. Walls and walls of Leonard's books. Several of the volumes were quite valuable. First editions of Freud, of Benjamin Rush, of Lister's essay on inflammation. A glass and mahogany bureau housed the sterling silver tea service that had once been Leonard's mother's. There was also a good share of kitsch: commemorative porcelain, bead bouquets, watercolor seascapes. The apartment's most interesting fixture—although of minimal commercial value—was a life-size plastic skeleton. It hung opposite the Laz-E-Boy recliner, where one expected to find a television set.

Abigail steered them into the dining room. She followed moments later with a tea pitcher and a plate of scones. "How long has it been, Wesley?" she asked. "You look spectacular."

"You do, too."

She poured the tea. "For a woman on the verge of death."

Bert and Wes exchanged looks. Abigail had always been a pale-skinned, curveless woman—but in a comely, country lass sort of way. Now she looked sallow and rigid like a tarnished candlestick.

"Take anything you want, by the way," she said. "I know there are some books that interested you, Bert. Help yourself."

"You know I can't do that," said Bert.

"Why not?" snapped Abigail.

Bert spooned sugar into his tea.

"I can't take them with me," Abigail persisted. "This isn't Ancient Egypt."

"You'll outlive us all yet," said Bert.

Abigail held her teacup only inches from her thin lips. "*No,*" she said. "*I won't.*"

Bert added another spoonful of sugar to his tea. He took a small sip. It was too sweet, noxious. This visit no longer seemed such a good idea. If he'd hoped Wes's presence was to have eased the situation—calmed his nerves, steeled his resolve—he should have known better. Emotionally, of course, Wes was on his side. But *rationally,* he remained neutral. That was the Alaska in him.

Live and let live. Or die and let die—as Abigail might quip. Wes hadn't taken Abigail to the high school prom, of course. He was less vested in her fate.

The truth was that, for nearly a month, Bert had been grasping at straws. Other men might have turned to religion, or psychiatry, or even the classics. These had never been part of his life. Instead, he'd become obsessed with the war news. He watched non-stop, religiously. Hoping the conflict might end. If there were no war, there would be nothing to protest. He'd also tracked down Abigail's son in Utah. First, Norman had hung up on him. When he phoned a second time, the son called him a shit-packing faggot. Bert saw no reason to mention this encounter to his ex-wife.

"Wes and I are thinking of traveling," said Bert.

Wes threw Bert a quizzical look. Abbie smiled. "That's terrific," she said. "You've certainly earned it."

"Does that mean . . . ?"

She shook her head. "I can work around your schedule."

Bert reached his hand into his trouser pocket and fumbled with his keys. His strong suit was property, not people. As hard as he tried, drawing any connection between Abigail and the bloodshed overseas seemed impossible. He also opposed the war, after all. Everybody opposed the war. It was something you opposed conceptually—like inequality or injustice. If they hit you, you hit back. He and Wes had rallied against the epidemic in the eighties. They'd marched for Matthew Shepard. They'd done their part. But for Abigail—who didn't own a television, who most likely couldn't name both of their United States senators—this was madness. He wanted to shake her. He wanted to tell her that she was the second most important person in his world. To say how empty his life would be without her jibes, her ravenous laugh.

Instead, he asked: "When?"

"Not just yet," said Abigail. "What is it they say after casting calls? Don't call us, we'll call you."

. . . . .

Abbie saw no need for immediate action. Occasionally, reading the names of fallen American servicemen in the morning newspaper, or contemplating the larger number of unreported foreign casualties, she was seized by a twinge of regret. Might she have saved these people? Had she cost some poor mother her son? But Abbie wasn't fool enough to believe that even her public burning could single-handedly alter national policy—that anything she'd have done would have mattered. Her goals were more modest, long-term. Also, she wasn't ready to die.

The first weeks of July, Abbie devoted to practical matters. She broke down her apartment as she'd done her classroom. Drawer by drawer, shelf by shelf. It amazed her how much junk she and Leonard had acquired over the years. A pair of pack rats. Now she gave it all away. The silver tea service and the medical books would go to Bert; she'd arranged it with the lawyer. Anything else of value—and who knew what had value these days!—was to be sold, the proceeds to St. Mary's. Abbie double-checked the perpetual upkeep on her parents' graves, gave the Dominican superintendent his Christmas tip on Bastille Day, bid silent farewell to her friends. Her death would be messy, explosive. She hoped to leave her affairs tied and tidy.

If anything scared her, it was the pain. At the age of eleven, she'd stuck a paperclip into an electric outlet. She still had a scar on her index finger. This, she feared, would be a thousand times worse. But as she learned more about Thích Quảng Đức and his Vietnamese monks, about Jan Palach in Wenceslas Square, she discovered that self-immolation—like most specialized skills— had its own complex artistry. You couldn't grit your teeth and bear it, as you might an injection. The trick, it appeared, was to lose yourself in a fugue state. One authority compared it to long-distance running. Through much of August, Abbie explored the subject. She sat in the small island of lindens and plane trees, at the juncture of Broadway and West End Avenue, reading about Afghan brides and Tibetan monks and the Ánanda Márga cult. If she'd had time—if life had taken a different course—she might have pursued these studies academically. She could already envision the shape of her dissertation: chapters on Joan of Arc, Indian sati rituals, Turkish Kurds. But Abbie knew she was growing weaker. She had trouble maintaining her balance, forming fists. Some days she didn't make it to the park or even out of her dressing gown. According to her oncologist, the cancer had spread to her brain.

Several times, Bert phoned. Dear Bert. "Just to check in." He wanted to discuss the war, but truthfully, the details of the fighting didn't interest her. She knew it was wrong. Deep down. *That* was what mattered. Why should she care for particular battles, the names of interchangeable generals? In college, she'd been rebuked for hazy thinking. Her history professor regarded her as pleasantly vapid. (Many years later, she'd run into the same professor at Tanglewood. *A second-grade teacher*, he'd said. *Important work*. She'd wanted to claw his eyes out.) If it were possible to miss anything once you were dead, she would miss Bert. His earnest decency, his tacky lavender handkerchiefs that looked like dinner napkins. And she'd miss children. Their tiny fingers, their solidarity. Being a second-rate classroom teacher, it was Abbie's great curse to love young children so terribly.

The morning after Labor Day, Abbie rose early. She'd stayed up late the night before, enjoying the final pages of *The Forsyte Saga*. (She'd read somewhere that John Hinckley and Mark Chapman had carried *The Catcher in the Rye* with them. Maybe, she'd told

Bert, she could inspire a new trend.) Outside, the air was damp. A nip of autumn already hung in the breeze. When Abbie arrived at St. Mary's, the children were already getting off the busses. One after another. In little yellow raincoats, carrying little brown bag lunches. The light was on in Abbie's classroom. Through the bars, she could see the walls layered with fresh construction paper. Orange. Green. Red. She walked to the pay telephone on the corner and called Bert.

It was time.

. . . . .

Bert picked Abigail up at the curbside. She wore tan slacks, a beige blouse, a matching kerchief. Her trademark canvas bag hung over one shoulder. She couldn't have weighed more than ninety pounds. On the phone, Abigail had warned him to expect the worst—but nothing could have braced him for the fragile steps, the bony cheeks, the sharp sinews exposed in her neck. Overnight, his ex-wife had suddenly become an old woman. A woman *beyond* a certain age. When she reached the car, he'd had to go around to help her close the door.

"Did you have any trouble?" she asked.

Bert considered lying, but he couldn't. He glanced in the rear-view mirror at the stack of press releases. These were to be distributed afterwards. The most critical resource, three canisters of gasoline, he'd concealed under a blanket in the trunk. "Smooth sailing," he said. "So far."

"I'm glad it's September," said Abigail. "I've always looked forward to September."

Bert started the ignition, but drove slowly. "We could stop for some coffee," he said, as casually as possible. "Wait for the weather to clear."

"Wait until I lose my resolve. Is that it?" Abigail rolled down her window and surveyed the rain with her palm. "Barely anything. Just a drizzle."

They eased their way down Broadway. Block by block, light by light. Both of them aware that Bert had chosen the slowest possible route. On the drive from Chatham Valley, he'd had so much to tell Abigail. About him. About her. About them. Now his mind had gone blank. "Wes said to send his love," he said.

"Please thank him for me. I always liked Wesley."

Traffic slowed around Columbus Circle. Jaywalkers darted through the intersection. Cabs honked. Abigail had selected the front steps of Federal Hall for her departure. Across from the Stock Exchange. The site of Washington's Farewell Address. She'd considered City Hall Park, Ground Zero. (It was like choosing a venue for a wedding, only cheaper.) Ultimately, she'd sought a place without children. A vacationing family, she'd feared, might break her nerve.

"Maybe we should have had kids," said Bert.

Abigail smiled. Her eyes glowed. "Maybe."

Bert considered reaching for her hand, but didn't.

After that, they rode in silence. Bert watched Abigail while they drove; she gazed out the window, her hands folded carefully in her lap. When they had finally reached the Financial District, she said, "In *War and Peace*, Pierre almost assassinates Napoleon. But, in the end, he doesn't have it in him."

They were stopped at a traffic light. Bert turned to face her. He expected to see tears in her eyes, but they were dry. "If I don't have it in me..." she said.

She looked at him helplessly; her hands were shaking.

"Hush," he said. "It will go fine."

. . . . .

The night before, Wes had painted the gasoline canisters black. From a distance, they looked like stereo speakers or lighting equipment. They parked illegally, and Bert carried the fuel up Wall Street. He walked slowly, so Abigail could keep pace. The rain had tapered off, leaving a residue of wet wrappers on the steps of Federal Hall. In one corner, a woman Abigail's age fed pigeons. A handful of "permanent" anti-war protestors stood entrenched behind a nearby police cordon. The lunchtime crowd was just beginning to file onto the streets.

"I'm not good at farewells," said Bert.

"Who is?" asked Abigail. She handed him her canvas bag.

Bert looked around aimlessly. The anti-war demonstrators across the plaza numbered about fifteen. Several wore tie-dyed t-shirts, shaggy beards. Others were better dressed, including one elderly man with a bowtie. They occasionally waved their political placards. Abigail nodded in their direction. "The competition," she said.

"For you," Bert said. "Absolutely no match."

Abigail smiled. She retrieved a tiny self-striker from a small rectangular box.

"The *perfect* match," she said, holding it up. "Now step back."

Abigail eased herself down to the steps and poured the gasoline over her head. First by tilting the canisters, then lifting them as they yielded weight. She might have been a small child enjoying a public bath. Bert couldn't bear to watch. He felt nauseous. He jostled his way along Wall Street toward Broadway.

Behind him, he heard shouting. He caught a glimpse of the flames reflected in the plate glass of a bakery window. It was done.

Bert continued walking, running. He headed through Battery Park, toward the water, the canyons of Lower Manhattan receding behind him. Songbirds flitted in the trees. Wes would have known their names. Across the harbor rose Ellis Island, The Statue of Liberty, New Jersey. Several small children were playing in the wet grass, illuminated by a thin white beam of sun. Bert stopped to watch them. It was a perfectly peaceful moment, the sort Abigail had treasured. You could close your eyes, and listen to the children's laughter, and imagine that nobody, anywhere, had ever died.

The Apprenticeship

······································

At the age of twelve, I decided—for no rational or explicable reason—that I wanted to become a tailor. This was the autumn we'd left New York for Southern California, and we were staying at my Uncle Lenny's ranch house in the Valley while my parents went hunting for a place of our own. My father made a point of always saying "the San Fernando Valley" in its entirety, like a man in the know—until a Bangladeshi realtor informed him a bit too politely that this was comparable to calling the phone company the American Telephone and Telegraph Corporation. After that, my father went out of his way to say "the Valley," in its more truncated form, at every opportunity. His radio advertisements all concluded: "That's the law offices of Carl G. Indursky, located in the heart of *the Valley*, just off 101 in Sherman Oaks." For years, even after he'd re-launched his political career on the West Coast, and won a seat on the Los Angeles City Council, nobody had the heart to tell him that referring to the Ventura Freeway as "101" rather than "*the* 101" was about as un-Californian as walking to work. When I insisted that I wanted to train as a tailor immediately, rather than wasting energy studying square roots and Ancient Egyptians, he sympathized. "What you say makes a lot of sense," he agreed. "I suppose a tailor doesn't need to know much about the Middle

Kingdom. But don't you think it's important to keep all your doors open?" When I persisted, he gave me a hug and promised it would never be too late to learn tailoring.

That's when I stopped eating. No fruit rollups. No frozen pizza. No coconut milkshakes at the In-N-Out Burger. Nearly two years before Bobby Sands starved himself to death on behalf of the Irish Republican Army, my "long-term Yom Kippur" drove the Bergman-Indursky household to its breaking point. My mother cajoled, begged, threatened. Then she took to her bed and survived on a diet of chocolate-coated orange peels. My Uncle Lenny, who operated a chain of private dialysis clinics, told me a story about a patient who'd once gone without food for six weeks in a frigid Chinese mineshaft and had to have his hands amputated. "How would you like to live without hands?" he demanded. I shrugged. "What's the point of having hands," I asked, "if I can't be a tailor?" On day five of my hunger strike, Uncle Lenny arranged an emergency appointment with a psychiatrist. The shrink, Dr. Glover, was a medical school classmate of my uncle's, a tubby fellow with short arms and particularly fat fingers. He began our interview by praising my mother's brother at great length.

"Are you married?" I asked.

"Yes, in fact, I am."

"Good."

Dr. Glover brandished his fountain pen over his legal pad like a scalpel. "Why is it *good* that I'm married?"

"It's just something my uncle says. That fat people in pairs look very jolly, but nothing is sadder than a fat person alone."

I'm not sure what Dr. Glover reported back to my parents, but the next day my father conceded that I might begin my apprenticeship as a tailor at once.

· · · · ·

The tailor shop where they sent me—after school, four days a week—belonged to Farzan Jafari, a kidney patient of my uncle's. It was located in the Silver Horseshoe Shopping Pavilion, a strip mall of twenty mom-and-pop stores anchored by a Wells Fargo branch office. Despite its name, the plaza was actually L-shaped. The third-side of the horseshoe housed a pair of large green dumpsters, a Salvation Army bin, and a lowslung police trailer with a cardboard sign reading "12th Precinct – Annex" taped to its siding. Local teenagers, mostly boys in camouflage fatigues with rat-tail haircuts, used the parapet opposite the bank's drive-thru lane for skateboarding. What a contrast they offered to the display in Jafari's front window, where father-and-son mannequins sported matching double-breasted three-piece suits. The "younger" mannequin stood with his arms at his sides while the "elder" examined a gold pocket watch. During my entire apprenticeship, the proprietor never once altered this display. Inside, the shop—as much a haberdashery as a traditional tailor's—was dimly lit and cluttered. The air smelled faintly of cigar smoke and naphthalene.

"So you wish to become a tailor," said Farzan Jafari. He was a short, dark, broad-faced man in his fifties, with bushy white eyebrows and a rather unsightly mole on his chin, but he spoke with an impeccable Oxford accent. Around his shoulders, he wore a measuring tape like a stole. "That is not an inconsequential decision, dear boy."

"Yes, Mr. Jafari," I agreed.

Jafari frowned. He slid the measuring tape off his neck and snapped it taut between his hands—as though he were planning to strangle me. "Are you telling me you *do* think it is an inconsequential decision?"

"No, Mr. Jafari."

"A tailor works hard for his bread, dear boy, that is true. But he has a trade, a craft. He is capable of making something with his hands. That is a great privilege." While he spoke, Jafari measured the length of my arms. "My father worked as a knife-sharpener. He went door-to-door with a treadle-driven grindstone. It took him nine years of savings to apprentice me out." Here, the tailor paused and dabbed the corners of his eyes with a lavender handkerchief—giving me time to wonder how much this arrangement was costing my own parents. "That a knife-sharpener's son might someday work on Savile Row. Truly a miracle. Do you know what Savile Row is, dear boy?"

I nodded vigorously. "That's the street in England where the king's tailors live."

"So you do know *something*. This might work out after all," said Jafari. "Are you certain you do not wish to become a solicitor?"

I had no idea how to answer this question. Luckily, a voice from behind a nearby tailor's dummy responded for me; it belonged to a slender young woman hemming a morning coat. "Please say lawyer, Papa. Or attorney. How many times have I told you? In America, solicitors are those dreadful people who phone during supper to sell holiday cruises and real estate in the desert."

My new employer waved his hand dismissively. "My daughter goes to night school for solicitors. *She* does not wish to be a tailor."

Jafari's attitude surprised me. In my own family, everyone knew that lawyers were far preferable to tailors.

The daughter, Raha, removed a pin from between her lips. "Papa refuses to accept that the world is a political place. He is happy in his ignorance, like the Emperor in his new suit of clothes."

Jafari recorded the length of my arms in a small leather-bound notepad. "How sharper than a serpent's tooth it is to have a thankless child. Shakespeare recognized that hundreds of years ago." He wrapped the measuring tape around my neck like a leash. "You won't be a thankless child, will you?"

"I hope not," I said.

"Good. Then we'll set you to work sorting buttons. I have a whole collection of buttons that have to be inventoried..."

"Okay," I said.

"Do you know how to sew on a button?"

I didn't answer.

"Well, after they're sorted, we might as well show you how to attach them."

"Thank you," I said.

Jafari noted down the width of my neck. "Any questions before you start?"

"Why did you leave Savile Row?"

This appeared to catch the tailor off-guard. "You're an impertinent little whelp, aren't you?" he asked—but with a grin.

"Yes, sir."

"Well, you won't be the first one around here," he added.

He removed a Mason jar of multicolored buttons from an upper shelf. Beside it rested another half dozen jars of multicolored buttons.

"So why did you leave Savile Row?" I asked again.

Jafari chuckled. "Too much politics," he said. "If you live in London for three generations, you can be British—*but never English*.... If you live in Los Angeles for three hours, you're already a Californian." Jafari appeared pleased with this answer. "Anything else, dear boy?"

"Why did you leave Iran?"

The tailor smiled. "Too many tailors."

. . . . .

Farzan Jafari turned out to be an exacting boss, but a kind one. Our relations were governed by one simple and overarching principle: His desire to transform me into a master craftsman. "If God can make a man from seven mounds of earth," he said, "I just might be able to do something with a nipper like you." To that end, I spent an entire month sewing straight lines into scrap fabric—first chain-stitches on a vintage Wilcox & Gibbs sewing machine, then lockstitches on a sleek Kenmore model. By October, I'd graduated to patterns. I did my work in a poorly ventilated back room, surrounded by water-warped copies of National Geographic and two women's hat boxes full of assorted zippers, but each evening around dusk, the tailor would invite me into his own equally disordered office for a cup of sweet tea. He served the tea in tiny glasses, yet poured his into a saucer before he tasted it. I did the same. Together, we dunked sugar cubes into the steaming *chaay* and then held them between our front teeth as we sipped. "I am supposed to transform you into a tailor," said Jafari, shaking his head. "Not a Persian." But he offered me a *nan-e gerdui* cookie made from cardamom and walnut flower.

While we enjoyed our snack, the tailor peppered me with questions: What were the consequences of a poorly wound bobbin? When were pinking shears preferable to scissors? How did the handwheel work? I'm not sure I have ever experienced such wholesome satisfaction as I did in identifying the three different models of presser feet. But after six weeks of quizzes, just when I felt confident that I'd mastered the ins-and-outs of machine sewing, Jafari summoned me to his office. He wore his most earnest expression. The tea service remained untouched on the shelf. He'd even shut off the cassette player that usually served up an eclectic mix of Gholam-Hossein Banan and Scott Joplin and Bing Crosby crooning *White Christmas*. When I entered, Jafari motioned for me to sit down in one of the hard leather chairs. He retrieved a patch of cloth from his desk and held it aloft.

"Is this your handicraft?" he demanded.

I looked sheepishly at the crescent-shaped design brocaded into the cotton rag.

"How bad is it?" I asked.

Jafari lit a cigar. He dropped the used match into his heavy jade ashtray, then rested the smoldering cigar on its brim. "Not *so* bad."

"But not so good," I offered.

"Yes, *so* good," said Jafari. "I am very pleased. It is *so* good I cannot tell it from my own work. You may be a brazen young urchin, but you're a darn promising craftsman."

"Thank you," I said. If the Los Angeles Dodgers had invited me to play shortstop in the World Series, I would not have been happier. I couldn't resist adding: "Never underestimate an impertinent whelp."

The tailor rested his interlocking hands on the desk blotter and drummed his fingertips together, drawing attention to his over-trimmed nails. He leaned forward and met my gaze. "You have learned a great amount during the last few weeks. Now, I must ask you to disregard absolutely all of it. Today, we will start from the beginning."

"I don't understand."

"I have taught you how to work the machine," said Jafari. "A master tailor works only by hand. A master tailor *never* uses a machine."

"But then why—?"

Jafari smiled. "If I had started you off sewing straight lines by hand, what would you have wanted?"

I didn't need to answer his question. He sensed from my expression that we'd both agreed upon the same answer—that I'd have asked to work on the machine.

"Precisely," said Jafari. "So it is fortunate that we have put all of that tomfoolery behind us. Now that we have removed the poison from your system, we are ready to roll up our sleeves and work."

· · · · ·

My new task—sewing straight lines by hand—did not require any stationary equipment, so I was free to labor on the main floor of the shop. This gave me an excuse to wear the baby-blue blazer with flared lapels that Jafari had presented to me. It also put me in closer proximity to the tailor's daughter, who up until that point I'd encountered only when passing to and from my interior workstation. I was too self-conscious to speak to her—she was in her twenties and wore low-cut blouses—but Raha Jafari quickly incorporated me into her ongoing battle with her father.

"Ask Cory here," she said. "What's your favorite restaurant?"

I looked up from my stitching. "In-N-Out Burger."

"See," said Raha. "Empirical evidence."

Her plan was for Jafari to sell the tailor shop and to open a fast-food franchise on the strip in Woodland Hills. When a customer was present, the pair interacted as properly as the butler and housekeeper at an English manor. Yet as soon as the door shut behind the departing client, an event announced by the jangle of a tiny brass bell, Raha wiped the colored chalk from her fingers and returned to her argument.

"You're on the wrong side of history, Papa. We live in a world of ready-made clothing—of T-shirts and dungarees..."

Jafari continued sewing the silk lining into a gentleman's overcoat. "You are entitled to your opinion."

"It's not opinion," persisted Raha. "It's fact. Tell him, Cory."

"Tell him what?" I asked.

"Tell him that nobody buys custom-fit anymore. Tell him that his grandchildren will look back on tailors the way we look back on blacksmiths and candle-makers."

The tailor sighed. "Is that so?"

"I only want what's best for you—for us," insisted Raha. "A fast-food franchise is like money in the bank."

"What do I know about cooking food?"

Raha rolled her eyes—mostly for my benefit. "You wouldn't *cook the food*, Papa. You'd manage things. You'd have an office."

"What I'd have," countered Jafari, "is an ulcer."

And on...and on...and on...

The other conflict between father and daughter stemmed from Raha's political endeavors. After work on Tuesdays and Thursdays, the tailor's daughter attended night classes at UCLA Law School; on Mondays and Wednesdays, she went door-to-door gathering signatures for a petition drive. Her organization, Free the Valley, wished to sponsor a ballot initiative on secession from the City of Los Angeles. Yet the tailor's name was not among the six thousand that the group had already amassed.

"Would it cost you *so much* to sign?" she asked.

Jafari held up a coarse thread and snipped it into two equal strands. "What reason do I have to sign? You are entitled to your opinion. I am perfectly happy to be part of Los Angeles. I *like* being part of Los Angeles."

"But the taxes, the services. It's not about *like* and *dislike*, Papa. You get back eighty-three cents in services for every tax dollar you pay to L.A."

"Do I?" said Jafari. "That means I'm only losing seventeen cents. That doesn't seem like so much to me—Certainly not worth all this politics."

"It's seventeen cents *per dollar.*" Raha drove a needle into her pin cushion. "And what's wrong with politics? You'd think after growing up in Tehran, you'd value your political rights."

"After growing up in Tehran, Miss Political Rights," said Jafari, "I know not to go signing my name about willy-nilly."

· · · · ·

One evening, after I'd carried three crates of men's gloves to the cellar and washed down the countertops, Raha asked if I wanted to accompany her on one of her signature drives. "I think it's time we start your political education," she said. "I wish I'd had my eyes opened at your age."

"Let the lad go home," objected Jafari. "He's just a kid. He'll want to be out-and-about with his friends."

Nothing could have been further from the truth—I didn't have any friends yet in L.A.—but I stared down into my hands. I felt bad about challenging my employer in front of his daughter. Moreover, I didn't want her to realize how unpopular I was in California. So she dropped the subject. But after Jafari dismissed me for the day, I called my mother from the payphone opposite the Wells Fargo and told her that I wouldn't need a ride home that day. Then I waited for the tailor's daughter in the parking lot.

Raha came out of the shop around six thirty, having changed from her calf-length skirt into a pair of tight-fitting acid-washed jeans. She'd also let her long charcoal hair fall free.

"Oh, you," she said. "Don't you want to go hang out with your friends?"

"I'd rather begin my political education," I said. "Have my eyes opened."

"I bet you would." The tailor's daughter unlocked the passenger door of her weather-beaten Plymouth. "Hop in."

I slid into the passenger seat. The floor was carpeted in diet soda cans and empty lipstick tubes and library books encased in glossy sheaths: Barry Goldwater's *Conscience of a Conservative*, Ayn Rand, *God and Man at Yale*.

"I'm a libertarian," said Raha. She sounded defensive.

"Okay," I said. I would have said the same if she'd been a monarchist or a follower of Jim Jones.

"Stick with me and I'll show you what's what."

So we drove from house to house along the wide, empty side streets of Van Nuys and Canoga Park and Tarzana. It was the week of Halloween—but a Southern California Halloween. Cardboard witches had been plastered on adobe shutters. Jack-o-lanterns leered beneath lime trees. At several of the homes we visited, we were mistaken for premature trick-or-treaters. They thought Raha was my mother! This part was so humiliating, that I actually felt relief when their doors closed in our faces.

"That's the most frustrating part of politics," explained Raha. "Watching people act against their own best interests."

"Why do they do that?"

"All sorts of reasons. Ignorance. Fear." We were stopped at a traffic light and Raha plucked her eyebrows with a tweezers while we waited. "Take my father, for instance. He's a coward."

"No, he's not," I snapped.

The car behind us honked. Raha readjusted the rearview mirror and hit the accelerator.

"I love him dearly, but he *is* a coward. . . . Papa has a double standard. He has nothing against politics. His problem is with *Iranians* in politics—because he thinks somebody will scapegoat us."

I could relate. That was how my uncle felt about Jews—why he didn't want my father running for office again.

"Do you know why we left London?" asked Raha.

"Too much politics."

"Too many Iranians," she retorted. "Papa was afraid of a backlash."

The tailor's daughter laughed as though this were the quaintest, most preposterous notion in the world.

. . . . .

Two weeks later, the Imam's Disciples stormed the American Embassy in Tehran and took fifty-two Americans hostage. Our family watched the events unfolding on the thirty-six inch color television in my parent's new *faux*-oak living room. Walter Cronkite in New York; Dan Rather in Washington. My Uncle Lenny, who'd come over to play backgammon with my father while Aunt Lily and my mother discussed various color schemes for the master bathroom, kept heckling the screen.

"That Ayatollah," he said. "It's a sorry day for the Jews."

Aunt Lily turned over a page in the album of tile-and-wallpaper designs. "For him, every day is a sorry day for the Jews."

"I'm just saying..."

"We know what you're saying," answered Aunt Lily. "Does it ever cross your mind that Jews aren't the only people this might affect?"

My father returned from the kitchen and handed Uncle Lenny a beer. "I hope none of this hurts your friend Jafari at all."

"Why would it?" asked my mother.

"You know how people are. Not everyone can distinguish between Iranians in Iran and Iranians here in the Valley," said my father. "Say, Cory, how are things going at the office?"

"Great," I said. "Mr. Jafari said I can start coming in on weekends and he'll teach me how to custom fit a suit."

Uncle Lenny turned to my father. "You wanted this," he said—over my head.

"Are you sure it's safe for him to keep working there, Carl?" asked my mother. "He's not in any danger, is he?"

"I'm sure it will be fine," my father answered. "We'll take things as they come."

Uncle Lenny switched off the television. "In Germany, they took things as they came. . . . This is a wake-up call."

Aunt Lily pointed her index finger decisively into the design album. "Go with the black marble, Fay," she said. "It won't show stains."

. . . . .

I'd expected the turbulent events on the television, which had provoked such a stir at home, to generate controversy at work as well, but at first the ongoing crisis had the opposite effect. Neither Raha nor her father made any reference to the hostages. They didn't argue much at all anymore—certainly not about politics. The tailor's daughter grew increasingly withdrawn. She abandoned her petition drive. When I asked her about disproportionate taxation, she bit her lip. "That was a mistake," she said. "A part of my false political consciousness." A pot-bellied official from Free the Valley appeared at the shop one afternoon and Raha dropped a thick stack of signatures into his arms. Then she locked herself in the back workroom for several hours. Jafari said nothing. The following morning, I helped the tailor's daughter scrape the bumper stickers off her car with hot water and a razor blade. So much for: "Moderation in Defense of Liberty is No Virtue" and "Ford-Reagan '76." When the last gummy specks of libertarianism had been scrubbed from the Plymouth, Raha replaced them with one sticker. Blue-on-white. IRANIAN. AMERICAN. PROUD. "Who the hell do they think they are?" she shouted, kicking a tire. Slowly, I pieced together what had happened. Raha hadn't given up her petition drive willingly. The organization had restricted her to a behind-the-scenes role, fearing that an Iranian representative might antagonize would-be supporters.

Nothing further was said of secession from Los Angeles. Instead of soliciting for signatures, I spent longer hours in the shop. One by one, Jafari revealed the secrets of his trade: how to cut a jacket pattern freehand, how to draft trousers with a square and stick, how to match the pinstripes through the shoulder seams of a bespoke coat. I studied the nuances of tweed, worsted, cashmere. I learned to sew with an open-ended thimble tied securely to my middle finger. After Thanksgiving, I was even permitted to undertake a project for a customer, a young boy's dinner jacket with corded silk facings. I had nearly completed the commission—I'd just finished sewing the jettings over the pockets—when Raha announced that she wouldn't be working that coming Saturday afternoon.

"And what is this about?" asked Jafari.

"I have a meeting," said Raha.

"A meeting?"

"Look," she answered sharply, "I can't be here."

The tailor removed his glasses and pinched the bridge of his nose. "You know I have my treatment on Saturday afternoons."

"I can't help it," said Raha.

Jafari ripped the rear seam out of a pair of wool slacks. "What meeting is so important that I should skip my dialysis? This is some sort of political gathering, isn't it?"

"You don't have to skip your dialysis. . . . Can't you go in the morning?"

"Can't I go in the morning?" echoed Jafari. "It's a health clinic, young lady, not a restaurant. You can't just show up when you please."

"I'm sorry, Papa," said Raha. "I'm sure you'll figure something out."

Jafari didn't say anything for minutes. He made a series of markings on the slacks with his triangular chalk. "I already have figured something out," he finally said. "I've figured out that you are *not* going to this meeting. I forbid it."

Raha squeezed her fists together. "Dammit, Papa. I'm twenty-six years old. You can't go forbidding me from doing things..."

"I *can* and I *will*."

"This is ridiculous, Papa. You're my father, not my owner."

"I'm not speaking as your father," snapped the tailor. "I'm speaking as your employer."

Jafari's anger reverberated through the shop. Even the mannequins in the window seemed to sense his mood—the "younger" appeared to be cringing and the "elder's" perfect grin now looked more like a grimace. A silence fell over the work-floor, punctuated by the snip of Raha's sheers.

I recognized this moment as my big opportunity.

"I have an idea," I said. "Maybe I could run the shop on Saturday afternoon, Mr. Jafari. That way you could go for your treatment and Raha could go to her meeting."

Jafari examined me intently. He placed his hand gently on my shoulder.

"Thank you," said the tailor. "Fortunately, that won't be necessary. Raha is going to be here on Saturday. Aren't you, Raha?"

"You're the employer," she answered.

Those were the last words Jafari and his daughter exchanged all week.

· · · · ·

One of the casualties of the mounting tension between Jafari and Raha was my own sartorial training. During an ordinary workday, the tailor examined my labor several times each hour;

it was unthinkable that I might cut through a bolt of Donegal tweed without his scrutiny and blessing. Yet that second week of December, he took minimal interest in my efforts. When I showed him my progress on the dinner jacket, he gave the garment a cursory glance and nodded indifferently. As a result, I managed to cut the buttonholes on the wrong side of the opening. I didn't have the courage to admit my mistake—particularly while my employer was under such strain—so I passed Thursday and Friday trying to look busy. Cutting scrap-fabric into the shapes of tiny rabbits and bears. Stitching and unstitching discarded sleeves. After the weekend, I figured, my employer would be calmer and my error more easily forgiven.

Saturday arrived with its usual surge of customers. A pair of middle-aged Vietnamese twins desired fitting for a joint wedding. A boy from my school came in for a Bar Mitzvah suit and we avoided each other uncomfortably. Around noon, the personal assistant of a professional golfer attempted to purchase two dozen custom-cut silk shirts—and Jafari had to apologize that he couldn't fill the order without first sizing up the man who was to wear them. No, he explained, written measurements would *not* do. The tailor kept referring to the golfer's assistant as a "valet." "Please tell your employer that I am sorry, but I cannot accept the estimates of an untrained valet. We just don't do things that way." The young man departed reluctantly, leaving the shop momentarily quiet. Jafari retrieved his fedora from the rack beside the wall mirror.

"I am going for my treatment now," he said.

Raha didn't answer. She was re-spooling thread.

"I trust you'll mind the empire while I'm gone," he said.

Still, Raha refused to acknowledge him.

"We'll be fine, Mr. Jafari," I said. "I'll keep an eye on things."

"I don't doubt you will," he answered.

The tailor looked at his daughter one final time, his entire body trembling with emotion, and he walked out the door. The tiny bell jingled.

"You can go to your meeting if you want to," I said. "I won't tell."

"I know you won't," Raha said. "Because you'll have a stake in our secret too."

I expected her to tell me that I'd be able to run the business in her absence.

"You can come to the meeting with me," she said. "It will be exciting."

. . . . .

The gathering took place at a twenty-four hour restaurant in San Clemente—nearly a two-hour drive away—and it didn't let out until six o'clock. That was long enough to establish three dozen working committees, devoted to everything from Persian-Hispanic Outreach to Neighborhood Security, as well as for a heated debate over whether to pass a resolution condemning the hostage taking. Some members insisted that such a measure was essential for the organization's credibility. Others wanted to focus solely on anti-discrimination efforts, to keep the group as apolitical as possible. Several factions threatened to splinter from the main caucus. In the end, the controversial proposal was tabled until the following weekend. The tailor's daughter, one of only three women at the meeting, was elected deputy secretary for public relations.

On the sidewalk, Raha kissed the other women on either cheek. She shook hands with each of the young men. "If only Papa could see this," she said to me. "He makes me so angry sometimes."

"You think he'll forgive us, don't you?"

"I don't need to be forgiven, dammit." Raha walked toward the parking lot, but stopped in front of a pay phone. "Call your mother and tell her you won't need a ride. Tell her we'll be out late."

I did as I was ordered. Then Raha drove us around the city for several hours, apparently with no destination in mind. We stopped for dinner at the In-N-Out Burger. She bought me a coconut shake *and* a Coke.

"Where are we going?" I asked.

"We're not going anywhere," she answered. "We're killing time."

I didn't press the issue further. Being with her felt like a date, so I wasn't complaining. It was nearly eleven when we pulled into the Silver Horseshoe plaza. All of the shops were closed. Even the windows of the police annex were dark. Raha eased the car alongside the front window of the tailor's shop and we stepped out into the clear evening. The pink-orange glow over the city rose over the eucalyptus trees. A hard breeze blew down from the hills.

"Do you know the game 'rock, paper, scissors'?" asked Raha.

"Yeah," I said. "You want to play?"

"I want to show you something," she answered.

I thought she might kiss me; I swallowed my gum just in case.

"Life is a lot like the game of rock, paper, scissors," she continued. "Sometimes hard work wins. That's Papa's approach— he's a scissors. . . . And sometimes paper wins. That's the way you learn how to do things in law school."

She lifted a hunk of jagged concrete from the traffic island.

"But then there are times when you need a rock," she said decisively. "The art of politics is figuring out when you need a scissors, and when you need paper, and when the only thing that will do the trick is a large stone."

Raha surveyed the empty parking lot. Then she lifted the chunk of concrete over her shoulder and launched it into the tailor's display window.

· · · · ·

When my mother dropped me off at Jafari's the next morning, two security specialists in white overalls were at work outside the shop. One stood on a ladder and measured the display window, periodically calling out numbers to his partner. The glass had been patched over with gray utility tape. Inside the shop, the tailor and his daughter were arguing, as they had done so frequently in the past, but with a sharper edge.

"This is not a solution," insisted Raha. "Do you really think a five thousand dollar alarmed gate can lock out the entire world?"

"I do not know," answered the tailor—his voice level, yet icy. "It can keep out sticks and stones. That's a start."

Raha jabbed her fist into the tailor's dummy as though it were a punching bag. "This is unbelievable," she cried. "So you just intend to forget about all of this—to pretend it never happened?"

"Yes, *please*. Let us *please* forget all of this," said the tailor. "I will forgive you for going to your meeting. We will have a new window. Everything will return to how it was before . . ."

Jafari sat at his workbench, his hands over his face, kneading his forehead anxiously with his fingertips. "I'm too old for this," muttered the tailor.

Raha paced across the work-floor.

"Goddammit!" she shouted. "You can't do this. Stand up and defend yourself, Papa. Before it's too late."

Jafari remained seated. "Enough," he said.

"It will never be enough," retorted Raha. She looked genuinely troubled for a moment—swept with indecision—and then she asked: "Do you know who threw that rock through the window? *Do you?*"

"I don't want to know," said Jafari. "Please. Enough."

"*I* did. I thought it might wake you up."

Jafari's head sunk further into his hands.

"How stupid could I have been? *Nothing* is ever going to wake you up!"

The tailor's daughter grabbed her purse and stormed across the shop. When the door slammed behind her, the brass bell came loose and ricocheted along the linoleum. The tailor sat motionless as an empty suit, his eyes resting on the heels of his palms.

"Does she truly take me for such a fool? Did she truly think I didn't know she was behind all this?"

"I had nothing to do with it," I pleaded. "I tried to stop her."

Jafari took note of me for the first time. "So be it," he said. "She'll be a solicitor. That's all there is to it..." He stood up and stretched his hands. "That means it's just the two of us from now on, dear boy. But we'll make a Savile Row tailor of you yet. I'm fairly certain of it."

I stared down at the floor.

"You do want to become a master tailor, *don't you?*"

"Maybe," I answered. "But I also want to keep all of my doors open."

Jafari nodded thoughtfully. "Yes, I suppose one should," he said. But he knew he didn't mean it, and I knew he didn't mean it, and that was the chasm that had opened between us forever.

The Other Sister

· ·

One morning shortly after the war ended—that same autumn their father drowned a litter of unwanted beagle puppies in the upstairs bathtub—Arnold Minton shook his two daughters awake with the tips of his fingers and announced that the girls were old enough to visit their grandparents. Or at least Sandy thought it had been the same summer. It was hard to be certain. She often suspected that people possessed two separate memories, one for public events like Hiroshima and the firing of General MacArthur, another for personal matters, and somehow her experiences of that morning had ended up stashed in the wrong category.

It should have been a short trip. Twenty minutes. Half an hour. (Sandy now knew a route through the municipal golf course that could cut it down to fifteen.) But that was before the days of DWI, back when driving drunk was a social *faux pas* akin to dining with one's elbows on the tabletop. So they got lost. Then they asked directions at a filling station, but didn't follow them, because "they didn't sound right." They circled the same landmarks: waterlogged scarecrows, gourds rotting on the vine. Jinelle rode with her arms folded across her chest. She'd scoured the girls and packaged them in dark muslin skirts, plaiting their hair in tight waves, but when they arrived at the cemetery, she refused to exit the Packard. The excursion had not been her idea and she was determined to convey her disapproval.

"Suit yourself," said Arnold.

"You know what I think," answered Jinelle.

(Later, after the separation, she grew more vocal in her criticism.

"Do you know what the problem with your father was?" she asked. "He was always very good, but he was never great."

"Very good is fine for some things," she explained. "A very good carpenter, sure. Even a very good doctor. My Papa, rest his soul, was a very good veterinarian. But a landscape painter? What the hell use is a very good painter?"

"How many *un*-great painters can you name?"

"I'll tell you how many. Only one. Adolf Hitler.")

Arnold's parents were buried under a coffin-shaped marble slab that reminded Sandy of a feeding trough for cattle. This was in the far corner of the cemetery, where the graves were old and huddled together like refugees. Through a chain-link fence, you could see the rear yards of the neighboring houses. Many of the porch lights remained lit. Damp yellow beech leaves cleaved to the slate paths and the soles of the girls' shoes.

"Sandy, Victoria," declared Arnold. His speech was resonant, oratorical, but slightly slurred, like Daniel Webster on a bender. "Allow me to introduce Mr. and Mrs. Josephus Minton."

Grandpa Minton had sold Fuller brushes door-to-door. Grandma Edith did piecework in a blanket factory. What money there was came from Jinelle's family.

"Now if you'll kindly step this way, ladies," continued Arnold. "I have another treat in store for you."

The damp air chapped Sandy's fingers. She'd never known her grandparents, so she wasn't sure how sad she ought to feel.

Arnold led the girls to a newer section of the cemetery. Here, chrysanthemums lined the broad gravel pathways and the "avenues" bore the names of fruit trees. The graves stood evenly spaced like tiny suburban fiefdoms. Arnold paused at a patch of empty grass near the intersection of Cherry and Walnut. With one fluid motion, he hoisted Victoria onto his shoulders.

"Observe, behold," said Arnold. "This is the hallowed scrap of earth where your mother and I will take up our eternal residence."

The gravesite was no bigger than a hopscotch grid. Someone had abandoned a mangled umbrella frame on Arnold's "hallowed scrap of earth," and a pair of grackles were mining the topsoil for breakfast. It was impossible to believe that anyone would actually be buried there.

"What's that?" asked Victoria, pointing.

Sandy stepped forward onto the damp grass. The small gray marker resembled a concrete hitching post, but it bore an iron "perpetual care" badge. *Oriana Grace Minton. April 3, 1937–April 9, 1937.* Victoria's twin.

Arnold grabbed Sandy, hard, by the back of her collar.

"That's nothing," he said. "Let's go home."

. . . . .

Fifty-two years later: Both Minton plots were now occupied—Jinelle's for three decades, Arnold's for three days—and Sandy had been office manager at the cemetery so long that she could locate individual graves for visitors without consulting the logbook. Temporary workers enjoyed quizzing her, flipping open the registry and asking, for example, where Maryann Lewis was interred, but Sandy would shoot back: Do you mean Maryann Lewis Died 1977 or Maryann Lewis Died 1984? When the temps inquired why she'd mastered what to them seemed a morbid parlor trick, or when a feature writer for the local newspaper delved into Sandy's motives, she always replied, "Busy hands are happy hands and an idle mind is the devil's workshop," which seemed satisfactory to everyone, although it wasn't quite clear how memorizing maps of the dead kept one's hands occupied. It was the sort of response people expected from a homely, church-going spinster. If she had explained her desire to preserve a living memory of the deceased—the way Jews consecrate the legacy of the holocaust—her inquisitors might have judged her cuckoo. Instead, they thought her upright, straight-shooting, knowledgeable, generous, witty, a lady of considerable spirit, but leading a life as lackluster as cold porridge. Which it often was.

And now Father was dead and Victoria was coming home. Victoria who had done nothing and gotten everything, while Sandy did everything and got nothing. Though you couldn't put it to folks that way.

—My sister's coming into town, you said.

—That must be a comfort. I do hope we'll meet her this time.

Then you had to explain that it wasn't Oriana, the mysterious and unseen Oriana with whom you occasionally toured Italy or cruised the Galapagos, but Victoria. Victoria, with her golden laughter and perfectly arched brow, for whom Allan Draper had jumped off the Jefferson Dam in the tenth grade. Victoria who'd had two stalkers in a single year of high school when you couldn't attract so much as a flasher. Victoria who'd gone off to Los Angeles, and appeared in a television commercial, and founded a talent and modeling agency with branch offices in Santa Barbara and Las Vegas, but sent home crates of navel oranges and cases of cabernet sauvignon, like a tourism agency gone berserk, when what you and father needed was cold hard cash. Though you couldn't say much of that either.

—My *other* sister, you said. The businesswoman. From California.

—For the funeral?

—Too late for the funeral, you said. You know how it is.

—Of course, of course. (Meaning: "We acknowledge there must be reasons why adult children don't attend their parents' funerals, but we cannot fathom what they are.")

—Oriana is on lemur-watching expedition in Madagascar, you added. Incommunicado.

—Probably better that you can't reach her. Why ruin her vacation? It won't change anything.

How strange it was, Sandy found, to speak of Victoria in these days following her father's death. Discussing her sister with the office staff, or her book club friends, or the Brazilian physical therapist, Eduardo, who was helping her with her hip, Sandy almost believed that *Victoria* was the fiction. Sandy knew everything of Oriana's life, because she'd cobbled it together from shards of fantasy. Her sister's whirlwind romances with titled aristocrats; the dinner parties at the Montparnasse townhouse; the safaris and archaeological digs and culinary tours in which Sandy was occasionally included. In contrast, Victoria appeared every five years or so, a different man on her elbow, her hair varying from platinum to onyx to henna. (She stayed just long enough to whet Father's appetite, to regain her perch as his favorite—while paying Sandy compliments that stung like insults, calling her "the good daughter" and "the loyal one.") When Victoria phoned, Sandy couldn't even picture the space from where she was phoning. It was out in the ether. An absolute blank.

Sandy had wondered—to the last—whether Victoria might surprise her with a cameo appearance at Father's funeral. It had been a short service. Attendance was light: a handful of Sandy's co-workers, paying respects to her and not to him. (Arnold's erratic outbursts had long since driven off his few surviving friends.) Sandy's pastor had contracted pneumonia and his surrogate, a divinity student from Hitchcock Seminary, stuttered dreadfully. He read a psalm and spoke of human fellowship. Having pumped Sandy for the crumbs of her father's life, during their walk from the parking lot, the poor boy forgot to include them. Not that it mattered. Sandy was the only mourner who'd actually known Arnold. As it was, she spent most of the service thinking of a beige jacket she'd worn to an interfaith roundtable the previous weekend. A reformed rabbi and a Buddhist scholar, both women in their thirties, had examined the morality of private property. Sandy feared she'd left the jacket at the church, draped over the back of her chair. Although she'd loved her father devoutly, far more than the old man was capable of loving anyone, anything, she was too depleted for grief.

Afterwards, Sandy hiked up to the contemplation gazebo. A low wooden bench lined four walls of the hexagon. Teenagers made out here, on weekend nights, blanketing the concrete floor with cigarette stubs and spent condoms. (She'd also found a noose one morning, hanging limp in the peonies.) Victoria had no doubt come to this knoll in her youth, as had Sandy, once, with Boyd Kelly, but nothing had happened between them. If you closed your eyes, you could see your whole life from there. It had not— despite what people often said—gone by so quickly. It had just gone by: demanding, haphazard, without traction. Sandy took a deep breath. *She could love Victoria. She could start from scratch— adopt what someone (Thomas Merton? Reinhold Niebuhr?) had called a hermeneutic of generosity. They were family, after all. Blood. After everything, she was still raring to love her sister. All Victoria had to do was to ask.*

. . . . .

Victoria arrived by cab two days later. Her hair was shoulder-length, chestnut and braided. She sported a long gray raincoat suited for a film noire heroine, dark sunglasses, and a turquoise scarf worn like Amelia Earhart. Hardly altered in five years. Even her dress size—*"Would you believe I still fit into a four?"*—remained constant.

The driver hauled Victoria's luggage onto the porch. Two large valises. A Gladstone bag. A ladies' hatbox streaked crimson-and-white like a candy cane. *Who in God's name still traveled with a hatbox?* Sandy spotted her sister through the dormer window in the attic. She'd been sorting through Father's effects, gathering threadbare suits for the Goodwill dumpster, airing out long-abandoned canvasses. *What a moment for Victoria to arrive!* Sandy did her best to wipe the sawdust off her knees before opening the door.

"Gracious!" declared Victoria. "I'm so glad I found you at home. I was terribly afraid you'd have gone off somewhere—to one of your church things—and I'd be stuck out here in the rain with my bags."

"I'm usually at work," answered Sandy. "Not this week, of course."

Victoria stepped into the foyer and removed her gloves. "Will you be a dear and help with my bags? I would, but with my back..."

Victoria had cracked her spine in high school. They'd gone apple picking and she'd fallen off the rear of the truck. An injury far less incapacitating, at the present, than Sandy's hip fracture. (Yet Victoria knew nothing of the hip—and it was easier to haul the luggage than to explain.)

"So good to be home," said Victoria. "It's overwhelming, almost. Each time the house seems somehow smaller. Dimmer."

She flicked the hall lights on and off like a realtor. "It's hard to imagine the old place with Father gone."

"That's *all* I can imagine," said Sandy.

The interior of the house had hardly changed since their childhood. They still used a chartreuse rotary phone, secured in a telephone cabinet. The same one-eyed rocking horse swayed in the parlor. Their garage and cellar remained cluttered with corroded farm implements. What a contrast to the exterior! The original six-acre tract—Jinelle's father and uncle raised squash for market—had been slashed and subdivided until the yard wasn't much larger than the house itself. A stately Tudor hemmed in by parvenu split-levels. Arnold had sacrificed the rest for gallery space, leisure time, food.

Sandy tugged the last of the suitcases across the threshold. Victoria had already passed into the parlor. She navigated the room as though visiting a museum, glossing her gaze over the alabaster bookends and the mantel clock and each commemorative plate. "Do tell me," she said, without turning around. "How was it? I mean at the end."

"It happened while I was in the shower," said Sandy, matter-of-fact. "He'd gone for a glass of milk and his legs must have come out from under him."

(A scotch and soda, more likely—but why tell it that way?)

"So it was sudden," persisted Victoria. "No last words?"

"I don't know. I don't think about it."

Victoria turned around without warning. "Of course not, darling. How insensitive of me—after all you've been through. At least one of us did her part."

Sandy squeezed her hands together behind her back. "How is business in California?" she asked.

Victoria's expression turned half-frown and half-wince. Sandy recognized the look: It was the same one mechanics and plumbers use when a woman asks about payment.

"It is what it is," said Victoria, shrugging. "In any case," she continued. "I have something for you." She rummaged through her handbag and retrieved a small package wrapped in brown paper. "Open it."

"You don't need to do this," said Sandy. She crossed into the dining room and, tentatively at first, poured a shot of scotch from the crystal decanter. (It was all hers now—no Father to measure the volume like a tide-keeper.)

"*I'll* unwrap it then," said Victoria. "I couldn't decide between the necklace and the earrings, so I bought them both. They're hand-crafted by this hundred-year-old Yuki Indian woman I discovered in Sausalito. She follows her tribe's ancestral patterns. Here, try them on."

"Later," said Sandy. The scotch warmed her throat and the tips of her ears. She could no longer remember the last time she'd indulged in hard liquor.

"The necklace is abalone with dentalium. Dentalium is a mollusk, for what it's worth. I always like to ask those things."

"Thank you," said Sandy.

"You'd never imagine what the earrings are made of. Take a guess."

Sandy had settled into Father's plush recliner. The chair looked toward the bay windows, so her sister couldn't see her face. She dropped one of the earrings into her scotch glass. It didn't matter to Sandy whether the jewelry was platinum or plutonium.

"Be a sport, darling," insisted Victoria. "One guess."

"Asbestos?"

"You haven't changed a bit," answered Victoria. "They're actually made from corn kernels. Pretty darn impressive, if you ask me."

Sandy swirled the earring around the glass with her pinkie. It amazed her that a woman possessing so little self-awareness—so little horse sense, to be honest—could run a lucrative business. "Corn?" she said. "They grow corn in Sausalito?"

"You're upset. Aren't you, dear?"

Sandy watched Victoria's reflection. Her sister approached the window and rested her hands on Sandy's shoulders. "You know I'm not good at this sort of thing," she said. "What do *I* know about bereavement and consolation and all that? That's always been *your* department. But I *am* sorry. Truly. If I did something wrong, that is. I do so want us to get along, darling. Really I do."

To Sandy, that seemed like *asking*. Or close enough. She reached back over her shoulder and covered Victoria's hand with her own. Both sisters remained silent. The poorly-oiled attic fan pulsed like a crippled heart. Thrub-dup. Thrub-dup. Outside, the gale slapped a rhododendron branch against the window panes.

Victoria finally spoke. "I'm going to miss it here."

"You'll come back to visit though, won't you."

Sandy was amazed at her own tenderness. How strange that a brief touch of flesh might obscure so much pain.

Victoria laughed. A laugh like the sleigh-bells of heaven. "Don't be foolish, dear," she said. "You weren't thinking of keeping the place, were you?"

"Leaving never crossed my mind."

How *could* she leave? The house fit her tight as a crustacean's shell.

"But we *have* to sell," said Victoria. "You do realize that it's half mine now. That Papa left it to *both of us*."

Sandy retracted her hand. She sensed her heart calcifying.

"You'll buy a condo in East Chatham," continued Victoria. "That's much more your speed. Do you really want to stay here with father's ghost in every closet?"

"I *live* here," said Sandy.

"I spoke to a lawyer," said Victoria. "He says we'd have to sell. If we ever went to court, that is—but I assured him that was nonsense."

"*I. Live. Here.*"

Sandy tried to blink away her tears. It was too much to process. Why was it that *everything* had to be taken from her? *Every last goddam thing.* She wasn't thinking of the house. She was thinking of her sister's fleeting affection.

"You have all that money," said Sandy, her words barely audible. "All that money..."

"I'm actually a little pressed right now," said Victoria. "Nothing serious, but a bit of ready cash could go a long way. Like a blood transfusion."

Sandy dangled the necklace in her scotch. If her sister noticed, she said nothing. *Victoria had consulted a lawyer? Didn't that make love impossible?*

"The more you think about it," said Victoria, "the more sense it will make. Trust me on this one." She squeezed Sandy's rigid shoulders. "Maybe I should drive into town for a bit and give you some space—I'll see which shops have turned over. I did just barge in here, didn't I? Is it alright if I borrow your car for a couple of hours?"

"Why *not* take it?" snapped Sandy "You've taken everything else. Take it and don't bring it back."

"I know it's hard," said Victoria. "I miss Father too."

Sandy said nothing, at first. She wanted everything to go away.

"The keys are in my purse," she said. "Just take them and go. Please."

She dug her fingernails into her palms and concentrated on long deep breaths, waiting to hear the garage door close behind her sister. She was on the verge of asphyxiating on her own throat—as though there were not enough air in the house for both of them.

. . . . .

Sandy remained at the window long after Victoria's departure. She sat motionless, except for her hands, which toyed with the hem of the brocade curtains. The rain let up. For an interval, a shaft of sun filtered through the rhododendrons, fashioning the dust mites into globular rainbows. Then a gray twilight descended over the room. Sandy's mood darkened with the shadows, until her thoughts turned ghastly. Or maybe they'd always been so. Her yarn-spinning was sin, she now recognized—not "sin" in the religious sense, a concept alien to her Unitarian skepticism, but "sin" as shorthand for the inexcusable. Oriana had died. Victoria had lived. To reincarnate her own Oriana, the quintessential un-Victoria, was implicitly to wish for the opposite.

And she did wish for the opposite. She didn't want to, but she did.

She'd begun innocently enough. On account of Boyd Kelly. (How naïve she'd once been! How ridiculous!) Boyd Kelly taught driving part time at Warren G. Harding Memorial High School. Wednesday and Friday afternoons. He wasn't particularly good-looking, or intelligent, or athletic, or generally noteworthy, except for one prematurely white lock feathering his auburn hair. That's how people knew him: "The guy with the white streak." Mild mannered, self-sufficient, forgettable. Boyd had landed the job, in part, because his father owned the cemetery: Its maze of service roads proved ideal for practical instruction. Boyd also managed the memorial park's books.

Through an autumn of lessons, Sandy hardly noticed him. She was embroiled with another boy, an oboist who kept her in a tizzy. (The boy knew nothing of the entanglement.) Enmeshed in this fantasy, she nearly steered the school's training car—a well-battered Nash—into a cenotaph. So Boyd Kelly. His firm hand diverting hers. Then the avalanche of hope: The crush. The cemetery job. The stroll to the gazebo. Such a glorious April morning that had been for romantic confessions! She'd stopped, she recalled, to savor the scent of a hyacinth. But there would be no confessions. No tender endearments, no hyperbolic pledges. What Boyd Kelly had wanted to tell her at the gazebo was absolutely nothing. (*How could it have been otherwise?*) He merely enjoyed the view. So she tried to entice him with tales of her exotic sister—living abroad with her mother's cousins. How could she have known, the afternoon he saved her from the cenotaph, that their hands would never touch again?

(*How could she not have known?!*)

Boyd Kelly joined the merchant marine and died young of a rare blood disorder. Sandy's creation continued to thrive.

Paris. Casablanca. Tashkent. Slowly, Oriana circumnavigated the globe. Sandy accompanied her with increasing frequency. She culled the details of her escapades from several water-warped Baedeker's guides in the cellar and the complete set of National Geographic Society magazines at the public library several towns away. (Around the same time, Arnold took to painting landscapes from picture postcards.) The trips abroad provided Sandy's life with a dash of color. They were genuine adventures in their own right, a blend of research and fancy that she came to relish immensely. Although she still set aside money for her grand tour, she did so only out of habit. Deep down, she sensed that her vacations with Oriana were far better than any she might take on her own.

Nobody ever doubted her. Not a soul. Who could? Mother was dead. Victoria had run off to California. Arnold cultivated a reputation for mania that kept the remainder of humanity at bay. Besides, Sandy was meticulous. She buttered herself in artificial tanner; she mastered basic Turkish phrases. If she claimed she'd explored caves in Cappadocia, where did anyone get off saying she hadn't?

(The assistant office manager at the cemetery, a gabby and insecure women named Francine Clamm, even insisted she'd met Oriana, briefly, on a train between Strasbourg and Cologne.)

One afternoon, seized with alarm, Sandy excavated two dense evergreen bushes from the yard and planted them around Oriana's grave, concealing the marker entirely.

It could so easily have been Victoria's grave. Her own life had been wrought by the difference.

. . . . .

Night fell with no sign of Victoria. One by one, the neighbors rounded up their dogs and their children. Downstairs lights snapped off; upstairs lights flickered on. The couple in the corner bungalow shouted themselves to exhaustion. Sandy paid no attention to the time. She helped herself to an additional scotch. And another. Like a wayward teenager left home unchaperoned. She didn't particularly want to get drunk, but drinking was something to do. Something easy, mindless. Sandy was already rather tipsy when the grandmother clock in the dining room struck eleven. Only then did she notice the length of her sister's absence.

It crossed her mind that Victoria might have died—caromed over the guardrail into the Shuckabee River. What then? She'd need to purchase a new car. In all other ways, her own life would continue as before.

Or maybe Victoria had taken her at her word. Driven off. Would she dare phone the police to report the vehicle stolen?

(*But that was claptrap! Her sister's bags still sat in the foyer.*)

Sandy realized what she was *not* doing. Negotiating. Pleading. Offering God sacrifices for her sister's survival—as she'd once done beside their mother's deathbed. *And why should she?* Let Victoria do her own bargaining.

Sandy retrieved some crackers and a hunk of cheddar cheese from the kitchen. She ensconced herself at the window, an afghan tucked over her knees, awaiting either her sister's return or the knock of state troopers in neoprene parkas. Whichever.

It was nearly three when Victoria finally appeared. Or at least the gaunt, ragged apparition resembled Victoria. (She'd taken Sandy's house keys as well as her car keys, so she let herself in.) Gone were her braids, her make-up, her pashmina scarf. And something inchoate was missing too—something as conspicuous as face paint, yet only noticeable in its absence.

"Good God!" gasped Sandy.

Victoria said nothing. She moved her gloves methodically and deposited them on the piano bench.

"What happened?"

Victoria seated herself beside her gloves. She leaned backwards, and the piano keys let out a low cacophonous clatter.

"I went for a long walk," said Victoria. "In the woods."

"Why?"

"Why the woods, dear. They seemed as good a place as any."

(How tired the "dear" sounded—thoroughly denuded of its condescension.)

"That was after I stopped by the cemetery," she said. "To take a look at Father's grave. Whatever you think, I loved him too."

"I never said differently," answered Sandy.

"You *think* differently."

Then Victoria related her visit to the cemetery. How she'd forgotten the plot location and Francis Clamm had looked it up in the log book. *Minton, Arnold. Minton, Jinelle. Minton, Oriana.* "You might imagine we had a rather long and interesting conversation about Minton, Oriana," said Victoria. "Is she still hunting for goddam lemmings in Madagascar?"

"Lemurs," said Sandy, reflexively.

"Lemurs," echoed Victoria. "That changes everything."

Victoria stared into her lap and pinched the bridge of her nose between her fingers. It had never entered Sandy's mind that her sister would be this upset. (Also in Sandy's thoughts was her own impending humiliation—the gusto with which Francis Clamm would expose her.) Why did Victoria even care? It cost her nothing.

"I have nothing to apologize for," Sandy said. "You've led your life. I've led mine. It's not as though *you* ever invited me anyplace."

"Is that how you see it?"

"How *else* should I see it?"

Sandy was about to say something further—something crueler—when she realized that her sister was crying. Silently, into her sleeve. But the tears did not last long. Victoria sat up abruptly, her back rigid as though braced for a firing squad. "I'm sorry you see it that way, dear," she said—her voice a passable replica of its old self. "I'm sorry you didn't appreciate the wine or the gourmet baskets or the glassware," she continued. "I had *thought* myself rather generous. I suspect *most people* would have thought me rather generous. But now the Mintons have never been most people, have they?" Victoria stood up, pounding out another racket on the piano keys. "Unless you have any further thoughts, dear," she said, "I think I shall retire."

Victoria retreated slowly toward the stairs.

Although Sandy was somewhat soused—maybe *because* of the scotch—she suddenly saw her sister with razor-sharp clarity. The mirage, once shattered, was unrecoverable. *How had she ever been so obtuse?* Whatever business ventures occupied Victoria in California, there could be no easy millions. A modest talent agency, maybe, possibly an extra alcove or storefront in Nevada. More likely a shoestring, letterhead enterprise that hardly paid the bills. (In the movies it would be an escort service or a house of prostitution, but this was not the movies.) The cabernet, the abalone necklace—it *had* been generous for a woman of Victoria's means. *But this was the most self-serving, pernicious variety of generosity. The offering that takes far more than it gives.*

For the only moment in her life, Sandy was without pity.

"One second," she said. "There is something else."

Victoria looked down from atop the stairs. "Yes, dear?"

"There is something else," Sandy said again. "In the spirit of honesty."

"I'm all for honestly," said Victoria.

"Papa did tell me one thing, at the end. About how Oriana died."

Sandy steadied herself the arm of a chair. She struggled to keep her voice level.

"He couldn't afford two babies," said Sandy. "They hadn't banked on twins. So he drowned her. Just like the puppies."

Victoria stood motionless for several seconds. Then she turned without a word and disappeared into her childhood bedroom.

"That's how Oriana died!" Sandy shouted after her. "He flipped a goddam coin!"

. . . . .

A full calendar year passed before Sandy returned to her parents' gravesite. The estate sold the house during that time, but nearly all of the proceeds went to satisfy Arnold's creditors. Sandy barely had enough left over to rent a small flat in a safe though shabby section of town. A third-floor walkup. The stairs exacerbated the pain in her hip. Scaling them came to involve such a commitment of time and energy that she avoided doing so more than once a day. But she continued on at the cemetery. She no longer spoke of either of her sisters. Nor did anybody else. To Sandy, at least. She suspected that her co-workers gossiped about her and probably thought her a bit cuckoo—but her reputation at the office concerned her far less than it once had. She still had her small joys: Church lectures. Book club. Showing off her memory to each new crop of temps. Yet she increasingly grew to see her life as something to be completed rather than treasured. Like a losing card hand that needed to be played through to the end.

And Victoria? They spoke often, at first, while the will passed through probate. Not so much as sisters as joint-owners of property. Then they spoke less. Sandy's lie about their sister had ruled out any future intimacy.

There had, of course, been no drowning. Even Father had limits.

Oriana's death had been slow and horrific and *entirely natural*. She'd been born without kidneys—condemned by fate from the start. In declaring otherwise, Sandy had surprised even herself.

When she finally visited the gravesite, she brought a shovel. The tool had belonged to Jinelle's father, or her uncle, and its wooden handle ended in a jagged shear. Sandy held it near the base and used it as a spade. Although the evergreens had prospered over the years, weaving a latticework of sinewy roots, they snapped easily under her onslaught. Eventually, the area around Oriana's grave had been entirely cleared of foliage. All that remained was the freshly churned soil. If you didn't read the headstone, you'd have thought it a recent burial.

On a whim, Sandy hiked up to the contemplation gazebo and discarded the shovel among the detritus of puppy love. She gazed down at the distant Minton graves. One large stone and one small one. "Behold," she said into the sharp morning air. "The eternal resting place of the Minton sisters." For, soon enough, there would be three small stones. It brought Sandy a perverse pleasure to think that, even from a short distance, visitors would not be able to tell them apart.

Before the Storm

· ·

"There is no such thing," says my father, "as a worst-case scenario."

It is September, 2004. We are crossing Lake Pontchartrain, between Metairie and St. Tammany Parish. The cypress silhouettes are receding behind us, wagging their heads in the breeze. There is no traffic, virtually no humidity. The causeway drifts to the horizon, where aquamarine water melts into cerulean sky, a tableau disturbed only by a flock of brown pelicans. *Even on a morning like this*, my father speaks of disasters.

"Consider," he says. "A head-on strike from a category five hurricane would bring with it a storm surge of thirty feet, maybe forty. You're talking a wall of water three stories high—enough to breach every levee downriver of Baton Rouge. You're talking submerged evacuation routes, people clawing each other's eyes out to get to the top of the cathedral. *Assuming there still is a cathedral.* Assuming all of Jackson Square isn't blown into the Garden District. That's a worst-case scenario, right?" My old man shakes his head. "Not hardly."

After a brief pause, to light his corncob pipe, he continues: "Terrorists—and I don't just mean Al Qaeda, but the Weather Underground or whoever—could use the cover of the storm to raid the nuclear reactors at Waterford and St. Francisville. That's *pounds* of uranium. You're talking a portable Three Mile Island, Chernobyl in a sack. And that's just for starters." He removes a handkerchief from his breast pocket and blows his nose. "Worst-case scenario?!" he says. "*Extinction* is a worst-case scenario."

My old man can go on like this for hours. He's a retired classics professor and the author of the three volume *Disaster Response in Antiquity*—a leading source on the Helike tidal wave and the Vesuvius eruption and every major calamity in between—so he also imagines himself an expert on contemporary threats to Western Civilization. I let him talk. He's sixty-six and enjoying what will likely be his last autumn of lucidity, saying his piece while he can still control his tongue.

. . . . .

We have already visited six assisted living facilities this week; Bonneville Park is the final home on our list. This sanctuary has been established on the site of an antebellum sugar plantation, and its administrative offices occupy the original Greek Revival manor house. A broad avenue leads to the mansion, sheltered by marble statuary and live oaks. Formal gardens of azalea and crape myrtle extend for acres, weaving around fountains and gazebos. The front doors open on sterling silver hinges. According to the brochure, portions of *Jezebel* and *Cat on a Hot Tin Roof* were filmed on the grounds. Yet being good enough for Bette Davis and Elizabeth Taylor is no guarantee for meeting my father's standards. He's already rejected homes with rooftop swimming pools and panoramic views of the Mississippi.

Our guide to Bonneville Park is Thad Faucheux. His official title is "admissions counselor"—as though my father were applying to LSU or Tulane. Thad can't be more than thirty-five, too young for his white flannel suit and heavy gold pocket watch. If he's aiming for the country squire look, he's missed his target. The man clearly works his upper body, but his frame still isn't broad enough for the part. Throw in his singsong voice, and his habit of pointing to things *with both hands simultaneously*, like a flight attendant, and Thad comes across as a youthful, gay mock-up of Mark Twain or Ben Matlock. "Good to finally meet you, Dr. Lefevre," he says, extending a bony hand. "And you must be Mr. Lefevre, Sr."

"I must be," says my father.

Thad flashes a plaster smile. "My name's Thad Faucheux," he says, articulating each word slowly, as though my old man were hard of hearing. He pronounces his name *Fō-shay*. "Your son and I spoke on the telephone." To emphasize this concept, he holds his fist beside his cheek—thumb poised at his ear, pinkie extended toward his mouth.

"You don't say," says my father.

"Do you happen to be related to the Lefevre who defended Fort Morgan during the war?" asks the guide.

"Not hardly," my father answers. "We're related to the Levine who changed his name to get into the state dental college."

I offer the counselor a sympathetic shrug.

My old man shuffles across the Victorian parlor, his gait wide and prancing, finally catching his balance on a gilded pier mirror. The jerking limbs and the difficulty stopping are distinctive of Huntington's chorea. This is the genetic brain disorder that killed the folksinger Woody Guthrie, that will soon kill my father. (I am adopted, so I will be spared.) He stands with his back to us, gazing out the palatial windows.

"If you'll come along, Mr. Lefevre," Thad says to my father, "we'll take a stroll around the campus."

"In a bit," says my father. "First, how's your drinking water?"

"Excuse me, sir?"

"Is it safe?" asks my father.

"The water?"

"Inspected?"

"I'm sure it is," says Thad. He appears a bit nonplussed, unhappy to be off-script. "Would you like a glass, Mr. Lefevre?"

"Consider," answers my father. "Water was the undoing of the Roman Empire. Why do you suppose Caligula appointed his horse a senator? Or Nero played his lyre atop Quirinal Hill while Rome burned below? Lead poisoning, that's why. Encephalopathy induced by contaminated drinking water."

"Bottled water is available in the cafeteria, Mr. Lefevre," offers Thad. "Evian, Poland Spring."

"That sheds a whole new light on Tiberius and his orgies, doesn't it?" demands my father. "And why Claudius impaled toddlers on pikes. So much for Gibbon with his marauding Goths and Vandals. Rome fell on account of faulty plumbing."

My old man turns to the guide, self-satisfied as Perry Mason. It's hard to picture him as anything other than my father, the man who once ferried me from okra-den to okra-den in search of the perfect gumbo with the same intransigence and intensity that now distinguish our search for a rest home. But to Thad Faucheux, I know, Ernie Lefevre is merely another unfortunate eccentric. My father's jacket is stained with grape soda, tomato sauce, raspberry sorbet. (You can read his entire week's diet off his lapels.) He's also grown out his silver hair, stopped trimming inside his ears. Today, his shirttails protrude from his fly. These miscues reflect his physical limitations, of course—but to our guide, he may just appear slovenly. When I look at my father, I can't help seeing an epic film. Thad Faucheux sees merely a still photograph.

"Dad," I say. "Mr. Faucheux's not interested in Roman water."

"Hmmph," says my father. "Well *I* am."

Our guide attempts to regain control of the scene, to return to his script. "If you'll step this way," he says, indicating a set of French doors with both his index fingers. We follow Thad across an enclosed porch and down a concrete ramp that, until recently, must have been a wooden stairway. A white-haired woman winks at us as we pass, then returns to watering a stand of chrysanthemums with a green plastic pitcher.

"You'll find that at Bonneville," Thad says, "we truly understand how much courage is involved in sacrificing one's independence." He sounds like a Confederate apologist, not a nursing home guide—but I hold my tongue. I desperately want this visit to go well: My father has been living with us for six months, frightening the children with prophesies of nuclear winter and apocalyptic meteor showers. He's driven my wife to the cusp of another breakdown. So that means no Civil War jokes, nothing to egg on my old man or ruffle our counselor's feathers. It's my job to listen while Thad does his hard sell, to play Jimmy Carter if necessary. "The sacrifice takes courage on the part of the patient," our guide says, "*and* courage on the part of the patient's loved ones."

"You want to talk about courage," interjects my father. "*I'll* tell you about courage. My boy and I—we braved Hurricane Camille in '69."

. . . . .

My father still speaks of Camille in the way combat veterans recall their battlefield heroics. It is his Thermopylae and his El Alamein and his Charge of the Light Brigade all rolled into one. For me, it is my earliest memory—a first splash of clarity in a sea of primordial darkness. I remember my father loading supplies into the lime green Chrysler Imperial he'd inherited from my grandfather: a barometer, his super 8 movie camera, several

mason jars full of prunes and pickled eel. I also remember my
mother—before the divorce—standing in the narrow driveway of
the house we rented on Burgundy Street, the wind pinning her
skirt to her ankles, beseeching my old man to come to his senses.
She shouted, she sobbed. She wrapped her arms around his legs.
When all else failed, she bashed in the windshield of the Chrysler
with the handle of a garden hoe. (Even today, recounting the story,
her voice quavers with rage.) If anything, her pleas just fed my old
man's determination. By noon, the two of us were heading up
Route 90 into Mississippi.

We drove past wind-whipped tung tree orchards, stray cattle
seeking shelter in a Catholic cemetery, two elderly black men
boarding up a liquor store. My father had to lean forward in his
seat to peer under the circular scars in the windshield. It was my
responsibility to hold his prune jar and his pipe. "Why is everybody
going in the other direction?" I asked.

"Because they're cowards," said my father.

"Is Mama a coward?" I asked.

My father spit a prune pit out the window. "Your grandfather
survived the flood of thirty-seven. *His* father made it through the
Galveston hurricane *and* the San Francisco earthquake. It's about
time we earned our stripes, isn't it?"

"What stripes?" I asked.

My father pounded his horn, swerving to avoid a meal sack
in the roadway. He flicked on the radio and tuned through the
stations. Nothing but evacuation orders, nautical forecasts. When
he finally found a soft music channel, it turned out they were
featuring a hurricane countdown. Billie Holliday's *Stormy Weather*.
Sinatra's *September in the Rain*. Joan Baez covering *Blowing in the
Wind*. At one point, the highway ended in a barricade of sawhorses:
National guard officers had commandeered both sides of the road

for outbound traffic. After that, I remember we drove several miles *in reverse*, on the shoulder, then cut onto a rural pike where my uncles had drag-raced as teenagers. We arrived in Biloxi during the early afternoon.

The town appeared surprisingly alive. Tradesmen in shirtsleeves darted across Main Street, bellowing orders into the breeze. Outside the theater, a crowd of teenagers had gathered to watch the proprietor remove the panels from the marquee. Nearby, a pharmacist struggled to unmoor his awning. Services had just concluded at the African Methodist Church, and we passed a young girl chasing after her mother's windnapped turquoise hat. Meanwhile, on Beach Boulevard, the breakers slapped against the sea wall. That's where we'd be staying, in a vacation bungalow just beyond the lighthouse. It belonged to one of my father's senior colleagues at Xavier.

"You ready for battle?" asked my father.

I shook my head. "I'm scared," I said.

"Scared," scoffed my father. "Do you think Cato was scared? Do you think Epaminondas was scared?" My father dropped the names of classical figures as though they were close personal friends. At the age of six, I imagined him sneaking off to the French Quarter for tête-à-têtes with mentors named Herodotus and Archimedes. "Do you think Pliny was afraid of lava?" he persisted. "Or Socrates of hemlock?"

"I guess not," I said.

"Stoicism, young man," said my father. "Show your mettle."

. . . . .

Thad Faucheux is too young to remember Camille. While my father boasts of our onetime bravery, the guide steers us under sycamores thick with Spanish moss. Wrought iron benches line the paths of Bonneville Park, evenly spaced like buoys. In fact, each has a large, color-coded number painted onto its concrete base. I suspect that this has been done to orient patients suffering from memory loss, but its effect is to create the aura of a playground— as if, after visiting hours, the inhabitants toss aside their canes and indulge in secret games of hopscotch. Not that we have encountered many residents. It is only nine-thirty a.m. Most of them, it turns out, are still in the dining hall.

"That building over there is the infirmary," Thad explains, indicating a low-slung stone structure that might have once been a carriage house. "The façade dates from 1834, but the insides are state-of-the-art. We have a full team of staff physicians. There's also a helipad out back. We can medevac you to the Ochsner Clinic in eleven minutes."

"How many helicopters do you have?" asks my father.

Our guide adjusts his jacket sleeves. He does this often, leaving dark thumbprints just above the cuffs. "We don't actually have the helicopters on site, Mr. Lefevre," Thad explains. "But we can bring them in at a moment's notice."

"That's good," agrees my father. He scratches the back of his head and yawns. "But the time it takes the helicopters to get here," he adds. "Is that included in the eleven minutes?"

"I can find out for you, Mr. Lefevre," says Thad.

"I'm sure you can," my father answers.

We've only walked a few yards farther, when my father stops short. "In emergency response," he declares, "timing is everything"

"Of course, Dad," I agree. "I'm sure Mr. Faucheux knows that."

"Maybe," retorts my old man. He sizes up our guide, sniffing as though purchasing an imported cheese. "Maybe not."

Thad sneaks a glance at his pocket watch. "Would you like to take a look at the living quarters?" he asks.

"Timing," continues my father. "Take, for instance, the Earthquake of 464. Before the Common Era, that is. The Spartans were caught unprepared. What was the result? The revolt of the Messenian helots. Yes, the same Messenian helots who fled to the Athenian camp at Pylos and helped Demosthenes trounce the Sphacteria." My father's face is crimson. "You may not care about this, *but it is important.*"

"Of course it is, Mr. Lefevre," says our guide. "History. If we don't learn it, we repeat it—right?"

My father nods, catching his breath. Thad takes advantage of the silence.

"These are the Cottages," says our guide. "Each resident has a private apartment with satellite television and wireless Internet access."

The Cottages are square, red-brick bunks. They're tidy, modern structures with petunias and geraniums in the window boxes, but they're no match for the manor house up on the ridge. I can't help thinking of slave cabins. I'm tempted to ask where the slave quarters actually stood, but I know this won't go over well. Besides, I'm confident our guide hasn't a clue.

"You'd be surprised," continues Thad, "how many of our residents surf the Internet. Not just the young ones, either. Twenty-four-hour nursing is also provided, of course, if and when it becomes necessary." Our guide detours from his script momentarily to wave at two figures approaching from the plantation building. "Looks like breakfast is over."

The newcomers are an elderly couple. The husband pushes a walker whose legs end in tennis balls. The wife wears a shield of political pins. They cover the gamut of the ideological spectrum. *Pro-Choice, Pro-Child* and *Abortion Stops a Beating Heart* rest side by side. Under *Kerry-Edwards 2004* sits *Democrats: Get Right With God.*

"Mrs. Beaufort makes political jewelry," whispers Thad. "She's harmless."

Thad exchanges greetings with the Beauforts. "This is Mr. Lefevre," he adds. "He's thinking of coming to live at Bonneville Park."

"So they've gotten you too, have they?" snaps the woman. "Resist, while the going is good."

Mr. Beaufort's eyes never leave the pavement. "Please, Gladys," he mutters.

And the couple passes on.

"They met here," says Thad. "That *does* happen."

Not promising, I think. After four wives, my father's past his quota.

"She's a character," our guide continues. "I've wondered what she did before she came to Bonneville, but I've never been able to get it out of her. I imagine she's always been a bit eccentric."

"Hmmph," retorts my old man. "That's like judging Carthage *after* the Romans had sown the fields with salt. Do you imagine Helen, at eighty, had a face to launch ships? Not hardly." He glares at our guide. "From meeting the likes of us, you'd never guess we survived a thunderstorm, much less a category five hurricane."

Once again—as more residents trek past us toward the Cottages—Camille takes center stage.

· · · · ·

The senior colleague who'd leant us his bungalow was a retired professor of horticulture. Outside, his foliage was unimpressive. Poinsettias. Cleyera. A pair of hangdog magnolias guarding the garage. Also, according to my father, a patch of marijuana out back. But he'd transformed the interior of the four room retreat into a veritable arboretum. Greenery shrouded all of the walls—

dieffenbachia, sansevieria, pothos vines. Glass cabinets housed rare orchids and bromeliads. Assorted cacti covered the kitchen counters, the linoleum floors of the bathroom, even the toilet lid. The professor apparently used his beachfront pad as an escape from the stresses of his domestic life, which explained the voluminous stacks of *National Geographic* and *American Heritage*, but also several gun magazines and large quantities of male-on-male pornography. The kitchen cabinets did not contain any cooking equipment. Instead, they held a nursery of dusty board games. *Parcheesi*. *Battleship*. Three different sets of *Monopoly*. The front windows had been boarded up before our arrival, but the glass doors to the lanai remained exposed.

My father explored the house, room by room. He tested the cedar support posts with his bare hands and grinned triumphantly. "Feel that," he ordered. "Solid wood. Straight off the lumberjack's axe." He kicked the molding with his boot. "If you want *that* these days, you have to build it yourself. Everything's hollow now, all prefab and modular homes." He retrieved a grocery bag from the sofa and scooped a slice of pickled eel from a jar. "Let's have a snack," he added, his mouth full of fish. "Then we'll get some boards over that glass."

The labor, as it turned out, took most of the afternoon. Whoever had paneled up the front windows had exhausted the stock of two-by-fours. All that remained was a stash of narrow wooden beams. These had to be applied one at a time. Many of the beams had rotted through and they crumbled easily under pressure, so my job was to sort the salvageable planks from the unsalvageable. My father did the nailing. Meanwhile, the skies darkened and the chandeliers flickered. Eventually, the power conked out. My father pulled the Chrysler alongside the bungalow and worked in the shaft of the headlights. He turned the radio on top volume—but all we could hear was the crackle of distant thunder. "Once we're done," he said. "We'll go inside and relax."

"Okay," I said.

"It'll be pretty snug, I imagine. Our own private Masada."

I snapped a corroded beam across my knee.

"I'm proud of you," he added. "You're not afraid of drowning, are you?"

"I don't think so," I said. Up until that moment, the possibility of drowning hadn't even crossed my consciousness. My fear had been broader, more inchoate. Now I had a specific threat upon which to focus. I ran periodically to the front-windows and peeked between the slats—watching the tide top the seawall and slosh into the roadbed. I'd brought my favorite stuffed zebra, Mr. Nobody, with me on the trip. Suddenly, I wished I'd left him in New Orleans. I didn't want him to drown.

My father nailed the last of the beams in place. "That should do it," he announced. He lit candles on the mantelpiece and windowsills, bathing the African violets and wandering jews in a soft orange glow. And then we relaxed. My father's idea of relaxing, of course, was all about history. I sat on a swiveling bar stool while he lectured me on the plague of Athens. That's right. While gale force winds ripped the utility poles out of their sockets, my old man narrated the death of Pericles. He paused only to light his pipe and to check the barometer. I used these interruptions to gauge the tide. Already, the surf was nipping at the base of the magnolias. The rain pelted the siding like buckshot.

"What are you looking at?" called my father. "I'm at the important part."

"Out there," I said. "There's a boat."

A long, narrow light was inching its way toward us. Only it wasn't a boat, it was a firetruck. Soon a man in a yellow raincoat emerged from the haze. He pounded on the window boards with the back of his flashlight. My father glanced at his watch. He popped a handful of prunes in his mouth. "What are you waiting for?" he asked. "There's someone knocking."

When I opened the door, the wind virtually blew our visitor into the hallway. He was a small, meaty man with short-cropped hair. He was wearing casual clothes, but a silver badge on his chest read DEPUTY SHERIFF HARRISON COUNTY—an emblem straight out of a John Wayne western. Water dripped from his every feature, and several seconds passed while he blinked the misery from his eyes. Together, we forced shut the door. At the same time, my father occupied the space behind me.

"I saw those headlights," said the deputy. "That was good thinking." He spoke with a syrupy drawl—hardly decipherable. "Never would have found you, otherwise."

"Maybe we didn't want to be found," said my father.

The deputy ignored him. "Is it just you two? I've got room in the cab for at least three."

"We're staying put," answered my old man. "I know my rights. There's no mandatory evacuation law in Mississippi."

The deputy blew on his hands. "Okay, mister," he said—his tone noticeably less friendly. "Know all the rights you want to. But sure thing says that you're gonna be shoulder deep in water in another six hours. They're saying the whole city might go under."

"Thanks for stopping by," said my father.

"Jesus, mister. At least let me take the boy."

I hugged Mr. Nobody to my chest and cried into his plush ears.

"James," said my father. "Do you want to leave?"

I said nothing. The bungalow shook violently, as though a cavalry charge were passing overhead. Urine began to trickle down my legs.

"I asked you a question," he persisted. "Are you going to brave it out like Leonidas or would you rather turn tail and leave?"

The deputy looked from me to my father to me again.

"I want to go home," I said. "Please, Daddy."

My father shook his head, visibly wounded. "Well you can't," he snapped.

. . . . .

Our guide flicks open his pocket watch. This is no longer a subtle peak, but a shameless statement. Instead of conducting us through the remainder of the facilities, he simply describes them to us: the renovated social hall, the bocce courts, the nationally-ranked rehabilitation center. Thad walks quickly while he speaks. My father's delays have clearly disrupted his timetable. I can't help thinking of my own obligations, of the outpatients whom I've rescheduled for the afternoon. As though to emphasize that our visit is rapidly drawing to a close, a bell tolls the hour. Ten o'clock. "The chapel is near the main building," explains Thad. "You probably saw it on your way in. We offer a late mass every morning, and ecumenical worship on Sundays." Over the gables of the manor house, the stone crest of the chapel is just visible. "Of course we have Hebrew services at well," adds Thad quickly. "Rabbi Hershman comes in from Slidell every other Saturday."

We are approaching the manor house. A family has rolled out a beach blanket under a maple tree, gathered around a middle-aged woman in a wheelchair. The woman's face appears swollen from steroids. A toddler sleeps on her lap. Two older girls, twins, play with the pump of a nearby well. It is all very idyllic, very Grandma Moses.

"What's your policy on guests?" I ask—less to learn the answer, more to remind my father that I intend to be a frequent visitor.

"Glad you asked," says Thad. "That's one feature that sets Bonneville apart. We offer continuous visiting hours. Twenty-four/seven. You want to show up at four a.m. on a Tuesday, that's your prerogative."

"Did you hear that, Dad?" I say. "Any time you want."

"The ancients viewed it as a privilege to visit the sick," says my father. "Not an obligation. Of course, they often viewed illness as a blessing. Consider epilepsy. The sacred disease. Responsible for the rise of Julius Caesar and Alexander of Macedon. Or take blindness. Nowadays, Tiresias wouldn't be revered. He'd be pitied." My old man steps toward out guide, looking up into his broad face. "Those were different times, of course. The ancients also didn't warehouse their elderly."

Our guide smiles blandly. "I'm sure they didn't, Mr. Lefevre," he says. He flicks a bit of pollen off his trousers.

"They had an organic understanding of illness," says me father. "Of disease and death as a natural part of life."

"Unquestionably," agrees Thad. "But didn't the Spartans drop their weaker children in buckets of ice water? Or something like that."

Score two points for our guide. Even my father is struck silent by this tidbit. He turns his back to us and pretends to relight his pipe.

"I was a history minor in college," says Thad. "Communications major, history minor. Good for job interviews. What's the expression? A little bit of knowledge is a dangerous thing."

"A disaster," mutters my father.

Our guide leads us back into the plantation house. Several other groups are waiting in the parlor, leafing through brochures and magazines. They all come in matching parent-child pairs.

"Do you have any questions, Dr. Lefevre?" Thad asks.

I shake his hand. "Thanks for having us," I say. "We'll think it over."

My father also shakes our guide's hand, but he doesn't say goodbye. He clears his throat several times and then shuffles and jerks toward the door. As I follow, I sense the other visitors eyeing me from behind. I'd like to think that they're sympathizing with me, but I know they're not. No. The children, I suspect, are condemning me—an oblique way of second-guessing themselves. The parents, of course, are far beyond that. They're deciding whether my father is the sort of man they'd want to die near.

· · · · ·

We walk in silence toward the far edge of the parking lot, yielding the plantation house space, as one might a theater after watching a harrowing film. The ground is paved with crushed shells and bits of coral. The shells crack audibly under our shoes. A lone mockingbird serenades us from atop a hedge of hibiscus. As we approach a pair of red picnic tables, my father stops walking. He steadies himself against the side of a large blue garbage dumpster. His face is twitching, another badge of his illness. The wide sycamore canopy makes him look small and fragile.

"So what did you think?" I ask. "Pretty upscale, no?"

My father lights his pipe. "He was in too much of a hurry," he says. "I don't think he liked me. Especially after I corrected him about the helicopters."

"You were only asking questions. Nothing wrong with that. Anyway, he's just some administrative flunky—you'll probably never have to see him, if you don't want to. The important thing is: What did you think of the place?"

"Sick people need time," he says. "I don't like to be rushed."

"I'm sure he didn't mean to rush you. And once you're settled in, you can make your own schedule."

I'm prepared to emphasize several of Bonneville's other promising features—the extensive library, the visiting lecturers—but my father's body is quivering. All of a sudden, there are tears in his eyes. "I didn't like it, James," he says. "You won't make me go there." He's asking, not telling.

I'm afraid I'm going to cry too. It's hard to accept that I have all the power now, this power that I don't want—power that I've never asked for. It's hard to accept that this is the same man who once held me on his shoulders, the waves lapping at his abdomen, shouting at me not to be afraid. "Spirits up," my father had ordered. "Think of Hector on the ramparts of Troy." Later, the water at his armpits: "What's the worst that might happen, James?" Atop the roof of the bungalow, watching the surf carry off Mr. Nobody, drowning *had* seemed like the worst-case scenario.

I'm older now than my father was then.

He is waiting for my answer, but I don't have one to give.

Iceberg Potential

. . . .

We had no Internet in my schooldays. Hager Heights Elementary did own two Commodore 64 computers, located side by side in the same fifth-grade classroom, and we spent much of that year coaxing pixelated turtles across their screens with rudimentary commands in Logo. How one teacher, square-toed Miss Harriot, had laid claim to both machines still remains a mystery to me, especially as the brittle spinster referred to the devices as "contraptions" and couldn't turn them on or off without help. I mention all of this for context, because these days a kid can type her teacher's name into Google and instantly strike a goldmine of demographic data, musical proclivities and even illicit conduct. I'll confess I have been doing that of late, both for my own teachers and my daughter's: Who'd have guessed, without the benefit of an obituary, that our school nurse, Mrs. Goldwasser, boasted ancestors on the Mayflower, or that Mr. Novotny, the gym teacher, and Mr. Pappas, the librarian, had been an item? Thirty-five years ago, all we knew of our educators was what they told us, complemented by what we witnessed ourselves, so the arrival of a new teacher like Stan Cadula proved occasion for girlish wonder and speculation.

We had expected Old Miss Swart for sixth grade—looked forward to her home-baked ginger cookies, dreaded the sight of the hirsute mole on her chin, braced for the odor of hard-boiled eggs that wafted between her discolored teeth and over the front-row desks. But Doris Swart had been forcibly retired that summer—her subsequent legal appeal endures online, detailing the district's concern for dementia—so we found ourselves welcomed after Labor Day by a lanky, bearded man of forty-five, sporting dungarees and a red-and-black checkered Oxford. Auburn hair sprouted from Stan Cadula's sleeves and his open collar. Once we'd all filtered into our seats—there were no assigned places, so I snagged a desk alongside my best friend Dana—Old Miss Swart's replacement perched himself atop the corner of his desk and strummed us to attention with chords on his acoustic guitar. Morning upon morning for five years, we'd inaugurated our day with the "Pledge of Allegiance" and "America the Beautiful." Grade six began with Stan Cadula channeling "Time in a Bottle."

"A fellow named Jim Croce wrote that tune," he concluded—speaking with a veteran performer's causal confidence, as though on stage at a concert, his fingers still dabbling with the strings. "I used to open for Jim before he passed on. Lovely man, Jimmy C. Salt of the earth."

I imagine girls a decade older than myself might have swooned to share a suburban classroom with a man who'd cruised blue highways on Jim Croce's tour bus—or, as he soon revealed, had shared an apartment with Richard Carpenter while dating the heartthrob's baby sister. But the musicians he'd grooved with through the seventies—Don McLean, Janis Ian, Peter, Paul & Mary—were as far removed from my pre-adolescent 1980s tastes as Bing Crosby and Frank Sinatra. What seized my imagination wasn't Cadula's B-list fame, or his lumberjack good looks, or even his silk-and-velvet voice, but his casual charm: Our new teacher was the most suave human being I have ever met—before or since. "We've got time for one more number," he announced. "And then we should take attendance." He fingered a few bars. "Here's a Gordon Lightfoot hit from 1971. 'If You Could Read My Mind.' We were up in Toronto one summer when Gordy put this ditty together..."

The classroom stood as silent as a concert hall—*more* silent. As though the whole building had frozen to the wistful pleas of Cadula's baritone, which wasn't far from the truth, because the other sixth-grade class, Mrs. Wilton's, was apparently listening through the walls. I uncapped a pink sharpie and penned a short note to Dana: *"I'm going to marry that man someday."* I'm still not sure to what degree I was joking.

I caught Dana's eye and passed the note across the aisle. As the frayed loose-leaf page slid from my fingers to hers, well below Stan Cadula's range of vision, a third hand clawed forward— like a raptor digging greedy talons through prey—and balled the paper into its fist. The steel grip belonged to a newcomer to our insular Hager Heights cohort, to a face marked by deep-set green eyes and a devil-may-care grin—unknown, yet also unsettlingly familiar. I watched in horror as the boy opened my note and tasted its contents, fearful he might read them aloud. Instead his grin exploded into outright laughter and he tossed the crumpled page back to Dana.

"What's so funny?" I snapped.

Stan Cadula frowned across the room at me, but continued singing.

"Nothing," the newcomer hissed between guffaws. "Nothing, really. Only if you marry *that man*, it will make you my stepmother."

. . . . .

Mrs. Wilton did not take well to Stan Cadula's morning performances, nor to the singalongs he mounted from the swing sets during recess. Yet what drew her to his classroom three weeks later was a more personal affront: She'd sent a student to borrow his overhead projector, because the bulb on hers had burnt out, and he detained the girl for nearly an hour—serenading her with Tony Orlando lyrics until she blushed. Nowadays, Cadula would likely have been fired on the spot, and maybe rightly so, but this was 1983, and having twelve-year-olds join a chorus of "Knock three times on the ceiling if you want me" was considered more idiosyncratic than corrupting. Except, that is, to Cadula's senior colleague, who appeared at his classroom door shortly after four o'clock, hands on her broad hips and eyes incendiary. She wore her iron-flecked hair in a tight bun, punctuated with a crochet needle, and to me she looked old as death itself, although she'd only turned fifty-four that summer—according to the online social security death index—a mere eight years older than I am now.

We'd contrived to stay after class that day, as we'd been doing almost every day since the start of school year. I sat beside Stan, soaking up his off-color touring tales and all-purpose life wisdom, while Dana flirted with Van Cadula over Nok Hockey or Chinese checkers at the rear of the classroom, both of us oblivious to the steady evaporation of our friendship. A sad tune from the seventies never strayed far from Stan's fingertips—each song a tribute to Van's mother, the willowy Haight Ashbury waitress-turned-groupie who'd run off with another band's bassist and later died of leukemia. Into this tableau marched Mrs. Wilton like the villainous lawman in a folk-rock ballad.

"A word with you, Mr. Cadula," she demanded.

She was one of those insecure teachers who addressed her colleagues by their surnames—like postal workers—and expected the same.

"Sure, Kay," replied Stan. "What's up?"

Mrs. Wilton appeared as though she might combust—and I resented her accordingly—although I realize, in hindsight, that she meant no harm. "A word *in private*, Mr. Cadula."

Stan lifted his guitar strap over his head and set the instrument down atop the desk. He followed his colleague into the corridor and she pushed the wooden door shut behind her, but it failed to close completely, so we heard the backbone of their encounter.

"Fifty-seven minutes," said Mrs. Wilton. "I was in the middle of my mathematics lesson and you kept me waiting fifty-seven minutes."

"Is that all?" said Stan. "Sorry. I lost track of time..."

"You lost track of time?" echoed Mrs. Wilton—indignant, incredulous, as though he'd lost track of the Hope Diamond or the nuclear football. "And when my boys and girls go off to college and can't calculate a percent, I'm sure it will console them to know that Mr. Cadula lost track of time."

"Jesus, Kay. It was only fifty-seven minutes..."

"And another thing. I'm not sure what your idea of age-appropriate is, but I'll not have my students hearing songs about bodies swaying and secret trysts..."

They went at it like this for another twenty minutes—Mrs. Wilton's voice rising, her complaints hopping from gripe to gripe, Stan unflappable and only mildly apologetic. When he returned to the classroom, he sported the same insouciant grin his son had worn when he'd snatched my note.

"Son of a bitch. That is one unpleasant lady," Stan said. "But I know her type. She may have a stick up her ass, but she's full of dirty secrets. You can just sense the evil lurking in her past—and, sooner or later, we'll figure out what it is."

. . . . .

So launched the war between sixth-grade teachers, an existential struggle that quickly unraveled the tightly-woven fabric of Hager Heights Elementary. Grievances mounted: Allegations, all true, that Stan Cadula used four-letter words, and claimed marijuana smoking was harmless, if done in moderation, and told Molly Armistead, after open school night, that her mother possessed "a nice set of knockers." Teachers chose sides—or, rather, teachers joined forces with Mrs. Wilton. Straight-laced Miss Harriot and toupee-tufted Mr. April and Dr. Krebs, the school psychologist, whose adult daughter later robbed a donut shop in Texas. Nobody took Stan Cadula's part, not publicly, although Miss Alvarado, who couldn't have been more than twenty-five and favored knee-length leather skirts, made a habit of popping into our classroom between lessons to chat. (She's Mrs. Clarkson now—fat as a distillery pig, my daughter reports—and she is *still* teaching second grade at Hager Heights.) The principal, a hapless, benevolent fellow named Maltstein, gave Stan Cadula a muddled "talking to," the main point of which was: "Some things are beyond my power." What precisely those things were, or what they meant for Stan, remained entirely opaque. Meanwhile, we continued to receive an eye-opening education, albeit one leagues beyond the scope of the formal curriculum.

Stan taught us how to pick a lock with a Diners Club card, how to communicate in Morse code, how to siphon gasoline during a crisis. He'd play "Alone Again" or "Cats in the Cradle" on his guitar until we had tears running down our cheeks, then serve up an ad-hoc lesson on the different types of electric current or the Reagan Administration's "shenanigans" in Nicaragua. Other days, he'd play soft rock on the radio and divulge war stories about the performers. Instinctively, we knew not to share these tidbits with our parents—although in my case, my mother and stepdad would likely have shrugged off their concerns and returned to bickering. If some of my classmates found Stan unnerving—and one, a Mormon kid named Bridger, did transfer classes—most of us worshipped the ground under his snakeskin boots. No Svengali or Rasputin has ever commanded such power over a troupe of sixth graders, and we'd have followed the man off a cliff, but he never asked for anything more than our interest and engagement.

We were ensconced in his classroom one early October afternoon—the red sun already low between the poplars opposite the schoolyard, bathing our tiny desks in a ruddy glow—when Albert Hammond's "It Never Rains in Southern California" drifted across the FM dial. Both Cadulas, father and son, looked up simultaneously.

"Tell them," said Van. "Come on, Dad."

"Tell them what?"

"That's my old man playing backup," said Van. "Song hit number 5 on the charts."

Stan shrugged. "Long time ago," he said.

I'd been begging Stan to bring in recordings of his own singles for weeks, so I latched onto each note with the need, the desperation, of a trapped miner listening for reciprocal tapping. And that Sunday, after Dana's father dropped us at the Laurendale Mall, I tried to purchase one of those albums at Vinyl & Vintage. The clerk—probably a college kid earning pocket cash—had never heard of Stan Cadula or Stan & The Crying Machine.

"You *must* have," I insisted. "He opened for Jim Croce and the Carpenters. He played backup for Albert Hammond."

"Albert Hammond we've got," said the clerk. "Aisle 4. Easy Listening."

I raced between pyramids of Jensen record players and racks of cassette tapes, navigating Jazz and Country and New Age 8-tracks;

then my fingers did the maneuvering, flipping past Arlo Guthrie and Frank Hamilton in a frenzy. Dana must have thought I'd snapped. But all of my doubts evaporated when I found Hammond's recording, the name "Stan Cadula" listed as a backup guitarist on the liner notes. The next day, I proudly displayed my find.

Stan appeared genuinely surprised. "You shouldn't have spent your money," he said. "I could have gotten you a free copy . . ."

"Does it really never rain in Southern California?" I asked.

"Rarely," replied Stan. "But when it does, it pours." He glanced across the empty desks to where his son and Dana were thumb wrestling. "You know what you've got, Kaely. You've got lots of iceberg potential. Never forget that. Just like Van's mother had. Mary Carpenter and Janis Ian too. Trust me. All you have to do is tap into it."

I felt stupid for not knowing. "What's iceberg potential?"

"You know how only 10 percent of an iceberg is above water," explained Stan. "All that other ice, the hidden ice, is lying beneath the surface—just waiting for its chance to sparkle in the sun . . . or sink a cruise ship. Does that make any sense?"

"Kind of," I said.

"It will make more sense someday," he added, wistful. "Maybe."

Then he dropped the subject of icebergs and launched into a diatribe against the FBI's efforts to shut down the American Indian Movement. He'd apparently met Leonard Peltier in the early '70s after a concert in Deadwood, South Dakota. "Nice guy," said Stan. "Couldn't carry a tune for the life of him, but he wasn't a killer." Stan shook his head, patted my knee. "You never know how life will turn out, Kaely. Got to enjoy the good times while they last."

I played that recording of "It Never Rains in Southern California" every night for a month, over and over again, until the tape wore out.

. . . . .

While I'd been fantasizing about my future marriage to Stan Cadula—a pipedream that involved him taking me on a nostalgia tour, introducing me as his wife to movie stars and European royalty—his son was making far more headway with Dana. The pair of them proved inseparable, increasingly rendering me a third wheel at the mall or the roller rink, despite their best efforts to include me in their plans. I suppose it was as much to impress my best friend, as to vindicate Stan Cadula, that I risked my life in Mrs. Wilton's cellar.

Van was the first to bring up the dungeon. I recall the moment vividly, all these years later: We were seated in a booth at Robustelli's Pizza, opposite the spiral gumball machine, debating whether we were too old for trick-or-treating, when Van said, "You know what I want to do on Halloween? I want to rescue Mrs. Wilton's daughter."

"Rescue her from what?" I asked.

"From Mrs. Wilton," said Van, grinning. He had one spidery hand draped over Dana's shoulder, the other lurking somewhere under the table. "Stan's been asking around and it turns out the old bitch used to have a daughter our age—but she was terribly disfigured and went to a special school. Nobody has seen her in years . . ."

I was in perpetual awe at how cavalierly Van called his father by his first name—without a hint of presumption—much as I still remain surprised that they'd ever allowed Stan to teach his son in the classroom. My own parents were "Mama" and "Papa" until the day they died.

"I don't get it. So she's at a special school . . ."

"That's what Mrs. Wilton *told* people. But Stan doesn't believe it. Stan thinks they keep the kid locked up at home—in a dungeon, more or less," said Van. "Another teacher knows someone whose friend's son goes to the same special school, and she says Mrs. Wilton's daughter never came back after second grade. Just vanished. Poof!"

Van snapped his fingers to emphasize the girl's disappearance. Dana rested her head against his shoulder, her eyes dreamy and a bit vacant—as though announcing to the world that she was too pretty to have to pay attention. (When I mentioned Mrs. Wilton to her at our twentieth reunion—the first time I'd spoken to her since high school—she hardly recognized the name.) We all waited in conspiratorial silence while Mr. Robustelli's nephew served our pizza and Dana's garden salad; then Van returned to formulating his scheme.

"If we free Mrs. Wilton's daughter, she'll tell the police how her mother has been holding her prisoner all these years, and Mr. Maltstein will have no choice but to fire her..." Van has his battle plan mapped out like a field marshal. "We'll do it on Halloween. That way we'll draw less attention—and, if we get caught, we can always claim we just were trick-or-treating... Or, worst comes to worst, that we were trying to steal candy..."

"Does your dad know about this?" I asked.

"Not exactly," said Van. "He can't—not officially—because *he* could get into real trouble. But he'd definitely approve. You've got to trust me on that."

Any doubts I had melted a moment later when Jim Croce's angelic voice crooned "Time in a Bottle" over Robustelli's croaky sound system.

· · · · ·

Our preparations commenced in earnest at Dana's house the following Saturday—my home environment had become too unstable for playdates, while the Cadulas shared a garden apartment in Marston Moor, more than forty minutes away by bike. (I'd almost gone to live with my own father in Minneapolis the previous summer, but then his fiancée had gotten pregnant.) While Dana's parents were at her younger brother's soccer practice, we looked up the Wiltons' address in the white pages— but the only options in Hager Heights were George and Timothy J., and we didn't yet know Mrs. Wilton's husband's name. "Why don't you call and ask for Kay?" suggested Van. "If she answers, or if it's the wrong number, hang up. Either way, we'll know which is theirs." Keep in mind this was long before the era of caller ID, and after a busy signal at George's, I instantly recognized the smoke-graveled voice at the end of Timothy J.'s line. Jackpot.

Later that week, we cased the house, an eccentric, three-story structure in the Queen Anne style shielded by laurel and privet. Set back from Beverley Road, on a ridge overlooking post-war bungalows and split-levels, the dwelling appeared as though it might indeed hold a dungeon, or even a medieval torture chamber, and while I was old enough to doubt the concept of suburban dungeons in principle, Van's confidence and Dana's vapid fidelity coupled with the structure's eerie baroque architecture to paper over my doubts. Cadula's son came armed for the occasion with a bolt cutter, a first aid kit, and a crowbar he'd pinched from the hardware store on Laurendale Boulevard. He'd drawn his long saffron hair back under a camouflage bandanna and shielded his eyes behind tinted aviator glasses. If he'd had the wherewithal, I have little doubt he'd have appropriated a shotgun for the occasion. Van Cadula was his father's son to the hide, lacking only the melancholy hue of loss, and when he pulled his bike up alongside Dana's and pressed his lips into her bare neck, I felt a twinge of jealousy course deep into my loins.

"What if she doesn't want to leave?" I asked.

Van squeezed Dana by the waist. "What's that?"

"What do we do if she won't come with us?" I asked. "Maybe the girl has been brainwashed so much that she'll want to stay."

This contingency had apparently not occurred to Van. He released Dana, then pulled his bike parallel to mine and spit into the undergrowth. The Wilton's house loomed above us like a gothic mansion, its upper floors aglow with yellow light. A cold front had washed through the night before and I could sense the autumn chill in my ears.

"Maybe she'll struggle against us," I added. "Claw at our eyes with her long nails."

"You've got a point," said Van, matter-of-fact. "We'd better bring along some rope."

. . . . .

Once we'd learned about Mrs. Wilton's daughter, we saw Stan Cadula's adversary in a far less charitable light. Her daily assaults—generally waged through proxies—struck us as the height of hypocrisy: What right did she have to object if Stan let us wander the hall without passes, or added a photo of Raquel Welch alongside Abraham Lincoln's and Martin Luther King Jr's on his corkboard, when she'd stiffed her own daughter of the most rudimentary education? Who even knew if the girl—whose name was unknown to us, but whom we took to calling Baby W—was able to read and write? We couldn't help wondering if Mrs. Wilton's allies knew her secret. It seemed doubtful. Whatever we thought of Dr. Womack, the one-eyed art teacher, or Mr. Hasenfusser, kindergarten, who later changed his name to Harper, or even Crazy Miss Riggio, who ended up civilly committed, and made the front page of the Hager Heights *Sentinel* for running up Davenport Avenue stark naked—not a pretty sight, I imagine—we couldn't fathom any of these adults condoning Mrs. Wilton's ongoing depravity. So they must not have known. Which was all the more reason, the argument went, for exposing their dastardly leader.

Did Van's father know of our plans in advance? At the time, I suspected he must have—maybe even that he'd planted the idea in his son's mind, which was certainly the impression that Van seemed intent to convey—but, in retrospect, I highly doubt it. Stan was far too savvy, I recognize in hindsight, to leave his reputation—his professional future—hanging in the hands of a trio of well-intentioned twelve-year-olds. Through October, he parried Kay Wilton's blows, several of which led to afterschool summits with dour men in herringbone suits, meetings which forced us from his room early, while he continued to ply us with torch songs and protest hymns and subversive theories about United States foreign policy. In class, we wrote letters to Soviet leader Yuri Andropov, asking him about his tastes in food and music. We took red pens to the *New York Times* and *Newsweek*, circling examples of right-wing bias. Between bouts of John Denver and Dr. Hook, we enjoyed off-color jokes about adulterous Sicilians. "Cadula's a Sicilian name," said Stan. "My Uncle Tony was the first Cadula in America—also the first Cadula to get into an honest business... He entered through the skylight." Another five years would pass before I understood why that joke was funny, another ten before I understood why it wasn't. But I laughed anyway—the whole class did—and Stan instructed us in rudimentary strategies for Texas hold 'em and seven-card stud. We'd hardly unpacked our summer camp duffels when Halloween roared in on a frosty breeze.

I insisted upon dressing up as an iceberg, about 90 percent of my body concealed under papier-mâché and chicken wire. I'd wanted Dana to accompany me as the Titanic, but Van arranged for them to go as his-and-hers outlaws; alas, Van dressed 1930s gangster and Dana in a western-style vest with a deputy's star, so they looked mismatched like Clyde Barrow and Calamity Jane. (When Van Cadula did stand trial twenty years later—for securities fraud—the media made hay of his double-breasted, chalk-striped suits tailored on Saville Row.) Someone that year went as Jerry Maltstein, with a placard reading PRINCIPAL draped around his neck, but sporting a bathrobe and slippers. And Molly Armistead decked herself up as an orange, her same identical citrus costume for the sixth year in a row. Among the teachers, Mr. Novotny dressed as Mr. Pappas, in his distinctive mauve turtleneck, while Mr. Pappas spoofed Mr. Novotny, carrying a baseball glove and a maroon doge ball. (Of course, they were a couple—how obvious now!) And Mrs. Turetsky, the school secretary, who seems to have vanished off the face of the Internet and the planet, unless I am grossly misspelling her name, appeared on stilts in a Los Angeles Lakers jersey—the whitest Kareem Abdul-Jabbar you'd ever set eyes on.

Stan Cadula greeted us that morning in a faux fur vest, fluorescent beads and flared turquoise pants, his head buried under a burgundy shag wig. One of my classmates guessed that he was Sonny Bono, another that he was a Martian. No dice.

"We give up," I cried. "Who are you?"

"I ask myself that every day, Kaely," said Stan. Then he laughed and added, "Oh, you mean *my costume*. Isn't that obvious? I'm my own former self."

· · · · ·

That night we shed the frivolous costumes in favor of dark sweat suits. Van managed to procure a trio of balaclavas, which lent us the appearance of stunted cat burglars; on any other night, we'd have drawn unwanted attention. "Even if we get caught inside her house," said our field marshal, "we'll just play it off as a prank. Who's going to arrest three twelve-year-olds dressed as cat burglars for trespassing on Halloween?" So we set out on our rescue mission, utterly blind to the absurdity of our earnestness. My mother and stepdad didn't even ask where I was headed, or with whom, only that I not wake them if I returned home late. They'd forgotten to purchase candy for trick-or-treaters that fall—much as they'd forgotten my birthday the previous August—so they planned to shut the downstairs lights and turn in early.

Van carried the crowbar and bolt cutter in a gym bag. We stashed the first aid kit and a coil of two-inch manila rope beneath a fleece blanket in the basket of my bike. Twilight descended as we reached Beverley Road—that soft suburban dusk that knells the close of another inconsequential day. The telephone poles had already been streaked with shaving cream, and here and there, a star-crossed egg lay shattered on the pavement. Once we had our bicycles stashed deep inside a grove of rhododendrons, Van led the way along the perimeter of the Wiltons' lawn and through the pachysandra that hemmed their back porch. I have no memory of fear, or courage, or excitement, only a spark of unshakeable determination—a sense that any hope of someday marrying Stan Cadula, or preserving a friendship with his son, and even with Dana, depended on the unfolding fate of Baby W. Yet I wasn't prepared for the cold-blooded crack of Van's crowbar shattering the cellar window.

"Take this, just in case," he ordered, shoving the bolt cutter into my hand.

"I'm going in first?" I asked.

"You have to. I'll never fit," said Van. He cleared the shards of glass from the window frame with his toe. "You've got to unlock the basement door for us."

Dana wore a dress three sizes smaller than mine, and her head towered only to Van's chin, but neither of us considered anointing her our vanguard. So what choice did I have? I squeezed through the iron casing, scratching my neck and shoulder; later, I'd realize my hoodie was caked to my flesh with dried blood. I'd already landed on the concrete floor of the Wilton's cellar when it struck me that what I needed was a flashlight, not a bolt cutter. But there was no turning back. From across the darkness rose an angry, irregular rattle—like a girl struggling against chains. I followed the thin beam of light to the cellar door, and soon Van and Dana stood beside me among the rusted lawn chairs and mildew. The rattling grew brisker, then stopped briefly, like a train discharging passengers, then picked up at a slower pace.

Van pointed—again nodding for me to lead. I shook my head, but whether he saw or not, he gave my back a firm push and then I was headed into the unforgiving shadows. As my eyes adjusted, I managed to navigate an ironing board and plastic garbage bags stuffed with surplus clothing—socks, undergarments, a button-barbed winter jacket. Around a sharp bend, beyond a wooden staircase, appeared a sliver of light. The noise had grown louder as we approached, now unmistakably the distinctive sound of chains jangling.

"I told you," whispered Van.

We paused in front of the light splinter. I braced myself, fulling convinced that Baby W would prove hostile to our visit—that she might indeed claw at my eyes. When I finally mustered the courage to pushed open the door, I found myself staring into the desperate eyes of a shackled, emaciated child—a creature hardly human in its suffering, yet simultaneously all too human—an image that slowly reshaped itself into that of Mrs. Wilton, in curlers, seated beside an electric washing machine. She had a book in one hand, and she closed it decisively as I entered, but she didn't appear either shocked or alarmed. The washing machine continued to rattle, some bolt loose deep inside its gut.

"My goodness," Mrs. Wilton declared. "What have we here?"

I dropped the bolt cutter and it clattered against the linoleum. All of our planned excuses evaporated from my memory like the dying notes of a love song. And then as quickly as my terror mounted, anger swept in—rage that this evil old woman had foiled our rescue.

"We're looking for your daughter," I cried. "We know what you've done to her!"

That was when the shock first appeared on Mrs. Wilton's face— an astonished agony, as though I'd stabbed her and then twisted the knife. "My God," she said. "My God," over and over again. And then Dr. Wilton was pushing past us, red-faced, blustery, tending to his unconscious wife and shouting for us to phone 9-1-1.

. . . . .

My mother and stepdad put aside their arguing long enough to ground me indefinitely, but the full consequences of our ill-fated mission emerged more gradually—in currents of analog, you might say. Although Mrs. Wilton phoned in sick the following morning, and the next, nearly a week passed before word circulated that she'd taken a long-term leave of absence. (At least, she'd only fainted; when the ambulance left, I'd been certain she was dead.) In her place appeared a dopey, patchouli-scented woman named Konstantino or Konstantinou who spent November and December fielding paper airplanes and muttering to herself in Greek. Both sixth-grade classes wrote Mrs. Wilton "get well" cards before Thanksgiving, and I signed. So did Van and Dana. The three of us were also required to write individual apologies to Dr. and Mrs. Wilton. By then, our entire class all knew what today we could have discovered with a few keystrokes: That Mrs. Wilton's seven-year-old daughter, Alyssa, had gone on a kayaking trip for special needs kids one summer and had choked to death on a leg of Dutch pretzel.

Dana and I hardly spoke during the ensuing investigation. As though by tacit understanding, we mutually abandoned Stan Cadula's lair—and if, during the next few days, he eyed us with chagrin when we raced out his classroom door at three o'clock, by the following week we'd been supplanted by Molly Armistead— who, after six years costumed as a polyester orange, held the distinction of becoming Van's final romantic conquest in Hager Heights. And then both Cadulas were gone, father and son. Poof! Not for singing of swaying bodies, or telling off-color jokes, or even invading the home of a grieving mother, but because Stan had forged his academic credentials when he'd applied for the post. Who had time to graduate from college, I overheard Mrs. Goldwasser jibe, when you're touring with Elvis and John Lennon?

The following fall we entered junior high and I fell in with an honors-class crowd that had little time for weekends at the mall or the roller rink. By Halloween of that year, I'd claimed a boyfriend of my own: A mop-haired eighth-grader named Ethan who kissed me for the first time in a New York City taxi after a Cyndi Lauper concert. I ruminated upon Stan Cadula with less urgency, and with less frequency, and finally almost never. Not until the week of our twentieth reunion did I think of plugging his name into the Internet, and I confess my heart suffered a jolt when I hit upon an obituary for "Stanley Cadula, Sideman to 70s Stars." But the accompanying photo and biography made clear that this illustrious Stan Cadula was not our Stan Cadula, not *my* Stan Cadula—just a hapless bystander with a not-too-uncommon name whose mention on a set of liner notes had once spawned another man's complex web of lies. I can't even say this surprised me. All along, I suppose, I'd sensed that Stan was largely a creation of his own imagination, and of ours, a conspiracy of fantasies, if you will. Part of us understood, even at age twelve, that we would never marry celebrity musicians or rescue captive children or remain best friends forever—or even live up to a fraction of our iceberg potential. We knew so little, yet so much.

Pay As You Go

· ·

The first thing you have to understand is how desperate I was—how desperate Gordon and I *both* were—because reliable homecare aides don't just blow in on an easterly wind like Mary Poppins. We'd already been having a hell of a time with Calliope, our thirteen-year-old, whose body had developed much more rapidly than her judgment. Then her younger sister, Andromache, passed through this morbid phase where she compiled scrapbooks of celebrity obituaries and insisted on trick-or-treating armed with a cardboard scythe. But if my father didn't exactly choose the best moment to fall down an airport escalator and hemorrhage into his gray matter, my mother didn't make things any easier by demanding that the homecare aide be a university-educated, culturally Jewish woman over forty, not too attractive, yet capable of handling Chopin's piano sonatas and reading Dante aloud in Italian. If she'd had her way, Mom would have included these requirements in her *Providence Journal* advertisement.

We finally compromised on a middle-aged Romanian widow named Raluca who'd run a hospital cafeteria under Ceauşescu. Since Mom wouldn't allow a stranger inside her apartment, we loaded my father into an ambulance and transported him to Midnight Harbor, where two muscular female EMTs set him up like medieval royalty on a semi-Fowler bed in our living room. The bus from Creve Coeur stopped only four blocks past our front door, at the beach access. My mother could visit every morning.

This arrangement lasted eleven days before Dad attempted to slit his caregiver's jugular veins. That was on a bright Saturday afternoon in early April. Gordon had taken the girls down to the water to test-fly a skyscraper-shaped kite that he'd acquired at silent auction during an AIDS fundraiser sponsored by the Institute of Architects. (One of my husband's most attractive, mystifying qualities has always been his appreciation for the simple truths of the universe: The elegant force of wind, the precise dynamic of billiard balls, the prismatic influence of sunlight upon oil.) Mom and I had the purchase orders and invoices from the jewelry shop sorted into neat piles on the kitchen table. We were still pretending that we could keep Dad's business afloat—at least *for the short term*—in case the course of my father's illness defied the consensus of modern neurology, but I don't think either of us really believed that he'd be capable of looking after himself again. A bit more lucidity, maybe a return of some motor function in his legs—at eighty-four, that was the best to be hoped for. But as I punched my father's platinum inventories into a pocket calculator, multiplying troy ounces against the closing COMEX price, we were interrupted by the splintering of wood and then panicked shouting in a foreign tongue, as though a horde of Cossacks had marauded through our living room.

My father had pinned the Romanian woman's ankles to the wall with his new electronic wheelchair; he brandished a jade-handled letter opener against the pendulous flesh beneath her chin. One of the homecare aide's knees protruded at an alarmingly unnatural angle, and she appeared to be in considerable pain.

"She's a thief," my father explained, his voice frightfully calm. Almost sociopathic. "Ask her what she's done with Papa's gold watch."

"I know nothing of watch. Nothing," pleaded the trapped woman.

"Oh, Abe," said my mother. "It's in the safe, honey. All of the watches are in the safe at the shop." She hurried across the room and placed her hand on my father's fragile shoulder, slowly lowering his unsteady arm. The Romanian widow limped to the sofa and inspected the bloody gash across her calf.

"I thought she'd taken it," said my father. Confused, ashamed.

My mother kissed his forehead. "I know you did."

That was the last of Raluca. She claimed my father had called her a *Gypsy whore*, and she demanded a full six months' salary, but since she didn't have working papers, we settled on three weeks' pay and the doctor bills for her ankle. After that came an obese Cape Verdean woman named Dulce Orlanda who sang Edith Piaf standards while she changed linens, and then a Haitian man in his forties, with a pointy white beard, who tried to sell Gordon on jointly opening a chain of tropical juice bars. But at some point, Dad, who passed most of his time napping and watching Court TV, accused each aide of pilfering his prized possessions. Roman coins; baroque candlesticks; first editions of Balzac and Leopardi. Once any caregiver had lost my father's trust, Dad couldn't tolerate her presence. He grew agitated, frantic. Often he appeared to believe that he was being robbed at gunpoint, that a brutal pistol-whipping was in the offing—these horrors having actually happened to him, during the summer of 1971—but it was difficult to understand how Mrs. Prout, the tiny, taciturn matron who'd replaced the would-be juice baron, could possibly have seemed a threat. Nonetheless, we were forced to let her go.

Nobody could have been as supportive through all of this as Gordon. He didn't complain about missing work, or paying off the disgruntled attendants, or the odor of diapers that could never be changed too quickly. Yet a coolness arose between us, a distance, because I sensed he thought Dad would fare better with institutional care—Gordon's own parents had lived six years at Hebrew Manor in Creve Coeur—while merely the word "nursing home" left my skin clammy. I found myself thinking back to a family vacation to New York City, when I was even younger than Andromache, and how Dad's boyhood friend, who'd risen to the position of chief buyer at Tiffany's, had led us through the jewelry vaults to see the precious gemstones. I'd trailed my tiny fingers through a drawer of freshly-cut emeralds, awed at the doors that my father's influence had the power to open. Now my daughter asked: "Is Grandpa going to die?" *Not if I can help it,* I wanted to shout. Instead, Gordon answered: "Your grandfather has led a rich, wonderful life." My husband didn't see the horror in Dad's decline—that's just not his nature—and a part of me couldn't help resenting him for this. I was secretly pleased with Andromache's next question: "If we're all going to die, what's the point of living?"

What was the point? Exactly.

So that was the state we were in when Trent Kendall signed on as our seventh homecare aide of the spring. Trent was a twenty-eight-year-old part-time graduate student in visual arts at the state university. He phoned about the *Journal* ad nearly a month after it had stopped running, and then appeared on the porch steps the following afternoon, with the yellowed newspaper folded under his arm. He was ready to start immediately, he explained. All of his belongings were inside his Plymouth station wagon, where he'd been sleeping for nearly a week. What Trent wanted in return was free lodging and a perch for painting the coastline. "It's a good deal, Abigail," he said. I was surprised at how easily he'd used my first name, but I honestly didn't mind. "You get a loyal, hardworking employee. I get an oceanfront view."

"I don't have three years' experience. Or current references," he conceded. "That's why I put off calling. But I spent two summers during college working at the Episcopal hospice over in Bayville, and I took good care of my own father while he was dying. Honestly. If he was still alive, he'd give me a top-notch letter of recommendation."

"Would he?" I asked, smiling.

"Look at it this way," answered Trent. "If I ever do make it as a painter, your little stretch of shoreline will be immortalized forever."

He rested one foot on the porch swing and gazed approvingly out across Narragansett Bay, as the encroaching shadows of dusk flickered over his delicately-sculpted features. I remember having two thoughts: That I was going to hire this young man—because he was the first applicant who was genuinely like us, *like me*; and that his looks would have been equally as attractive on a woman.

Maybe because of Trent's candor, I felt obliged to warn him upfront what a challenge caring for my father would be. "You have to be alert at all times," I explained. "He whacked the last aide in the forehead with his dentures."

"I paint watercolor seascapes for a living," Trent answered. "I'll take the risk."

Something about the way he said this—the good-hearted innocence of it—made me want to reach forward and touch his sleeve. Not in a romantic way, not yet, but more as a tainted mortal might reach for the arm of a saint. I'd been a struggling actress once, before I'd met Gordon, before I'd moved back to Rhode Island and "made do" with reviewing foreign films for the *Creve Coeur Sentinel*. I knew all about answering ads for babysitting jobs—and wading knee-deep into other people's bullshit. The only difference between me and Trent Kendall was that I'd already accepted life's script, while he was still fighting against it. That's what happens between twenty-eight and forty-three.

"So when can I meet the holiest of terrors?" asked Trent.

I realized I'd been staring, and I looked away quickly.

Inside the living room, the air stank of pine-scented freshener. Both of the ceiling bulbs had burnt out, leaving only the table lamp to illuminate the makeshift sanitarium. Dad sat beside the bay window with the curtains drawn. He held a clock radio on his lap, listening to Glenn Miller hit the high notes in "Tuxedo Junction." Across the room, Monty Hall offered contestants a choice of instant cash or the prize behind Door Number 3. My father didn't even look up until we crossed in front of the television. When he did, I noticed that one of his eyes was bloodshot.

"What does *he* want?" demanded my father.

I didn't have a chance to answer.

"I'm glad to meet you, Mr. Hartman," said Trent. "I'm your new bodyguard."

That pleased my father. "It's about time," he said. "You can't fall asleep around here without someone trying to rob you blind."

Dad lowered the radio volume. To my surprise, he even shook Trent's hand.

"That's what I'm here for," Trent said. "So you can rest worry-free."

"I sure do hope so. I had to sleep with my hands inside the pillowcase, or that last fellow would have had the ring off my finger." My father proudly displayed this artifact of his masonic service. Then his free hand tightened suddenly on the arm of the wheelchair, as though he'd been jabbed with a bayonet. "Say, are you bonded?"

"Bonded and insured," Trent lied. "Your daughter has all the paperwork."

"Then you're hired," said Dad. "Congratulations."

And with that pronouncement, my father closed his eyes and dozed off.

When he woke up several hours later, he immediately called for his bodyguard. I summoned Trent from the veranda, where he'd been sketching the twilight in charcoal, and Dad berated him for abandoning his post. "I'm depending on you, young man. Don't let me down," he said. "My life could depend upon it." From that first day onward, he couldn't relax without his aide's nearly continuous protection.

Trent's easygoing cheer rapidly overtook the entire household. Calliope pleaded for him to let her model, and he eventually painted her portrait in acrylics, although he adamantly refused to let her pose in the nude. Then Andromache, whose terror that we might all die suddenly, leaving her to fend for herself, made each day of third grade a continuous torment, declared that she was no longer afraid of being orphaned. That night, Gordon and I had sex for the first time in months.

Even my mother—although displeased with the bodyguard ruse—found our new attendant disarming. She took to calling him Boy Wonder. "Your father seems so much calmer these last few days," she confessed on the drive back from the business broker's, where we'd contracted to unload the jewelry shop. "But I think he's a homosexual. I don't know why I didn't see that much sooner."

It took me a moment to realize she meant Trent and not my father.

"Why should it matter if he's gay?" I demanded. "Anyway, he's not."

The truth was that I knew nothing of our attendant's personal life.

My mother shrugged. "I'm just saying," she said.

It was shortly afterwards that our valuables started disappearing.

. . . . .

The first item I noticed missing was a set of black pearls that Gordon had given me on our tenth wedding anniversary. I've never been one for wearing much jewelry—maybe this is some form of subtle rebellion against my parents—and the few expensive pieces that I do own, diamond and sapphire mementos of my late mother-in-law, I keep stored in the safe deposit box alongside our wills and savings bonds. I imagine that's how Calliope and Andromache will find them in fifty years. But when Dad didn't recover after his surgery, Mom suggested taking a few of his personal treasures out of the shop safe and stashing them away for the girls, beyond the IRS's reach. She picked out the pieces: Grandma Bessie's engagement ring, matching white-gold lockets, a pair of ruby earrings that had once belonged to Nathaniel Hawthorne's daughter. I carried the trove from the shop to the bank in my handbag, sobbing during the drive. When I opened our box—it took me several minutes to remember the ID number—I rediscovered the pearl necklace, and, on a whim, I brought it home to wear for my Vassar reunion. I could have sworn I'd left it in the leather-and-ormolu jewelry case on my bedroom bureau. It never crossed my mind that someone might steal it. But on the night before we left for Poughkeepsie, all that remained in the case were barrettes and bobby pins.

My initial reaction was to blame myself. Misplacing the necklace would certainly not have been the first harebrained blunder I'd managed while under the stress of looking after my father. Only a few weeks earlier, I'd mailed the mortgage payment without stamping the envelope; I'd also written Calliope a seventeen-dollar check to pay for her class field trip to the whaling museum on Conanicut Island—and, without thinking, I'd endorsed it. So when we scoured the house from attic to cellar, and the pearls didn't turn up, Gordon wasn't terribly alarmed. "You'll find them soon enough," he assured me. "Under the ice trays or inside the piano bench or someplace like that. If we're lucky, you'll find my unmatched socks with them." I knew he was wrong, of course. In my neurotic state, I'd *already* checked inside the piano bench and under the ice trays. (It's amazing to me how upset I was to lose a necklace that I hadn't thought about even once in nearly five years, but a burr inside my stocking could not have been more frustrating.) Fortunately, an evening of dinner and dancing with my college suitemates, one of whom actually had become a marginally successfully Broadway actress, helped to sooth my nerves. Gordon and I took turns praising Trent Kendall on the drive home. I'd phoned him three times that night, to check up on my father. If the Romanian battle-axe had still been with us, I would never have dared to leave the state.

Two days later, as I attempted to elevate Dad's bed, so he wouldn't roll off during the night, I caught my middle three fingers under the steel frame. I immediately removed my wedding band, knowing that all the waters of the Arctic couldn't keep my hand from swelling. Trent was in the kitchen when I injured myself, rinsing his brushes in the industrial sink opposite the pantry. He'd enlisted Andromache to help him scrub, and my daughter was actually giggling, for the first time in many months, while Trent told her how the Shakers had rocked their elderly to death in adult-sized cradles. I pushed past them apologetically, bathing my wounds under the tap. At the same time, I sent Andromache for my purse, and dropped the engraved band loose inside. Trent Kendall pressed a cloth-wrapped ice cube against my cuticles for several minutes. "I know that's not fun," he said. "But you'll be glad to still have those nails tomorrow." Then he gently swaddled my hand in gauze, a maneuver both intimate and clinical. The following evening, when I'd finally recovered enough to replace my ring, it was gone.

Once again, I searched behind the refrigerator and ransacked the cutlery drawers, but this time I was confident that I'd left the ring inside my purse. Even as I retraced my steps of the previous twenty-four hours, jostling my memory for the entranced moment when I'd unconsciously buried the gold band beneath the azalea hedge, my suspicions were gelling into certainty: Mom's Boy Wonder was a common thief. What a fool I'd been to hire him without references! These days, *anybody* can get references. Besides, I remembered what it was like to be a cash-strapped artist granted free reign in an upscale home. I'd never stolen anything myself, but I had been sorely tempted.

Gordon had accompanied the girls sailing that afternoon— he'd bought himself a used sunfish for his forty-fifth birthday— but I decided not to wait for his return. Instead, I stormed into the living room to confront our light-fingered employee. Trent stood beside Dad's bed, feeding him yogurt. My mother sat ensconced on the sofa, her legs sheltered by a hand-crocheted afghan, relating a story about growing up in Jewish Antwerp before the war—these were the only stories she ever told—while Trent nodded along sympathetically. I watched from the entryway, waiting for a break in her narrative. When Mom finally paused to sip water from a plastic cup, Trent spoke before I could.

"Your mother is quite a raconteur," he said. "She should really write a memoir."

My mother blushed. "We've got a flatterer, Abby. That's what I like about him."

Trent lowered the yogurt spoon and dabbed my father's lips with a dishtowel. Dad stared past us, into the plaster. One of his bad days.

"You look upset, Abigail," said Trent. "Is something wrong?"

He asked so innocently, so compassionately, that I lost the nerve to accuse him directly. What if I were wrong, I wondered, even though I knew I was right. I should have waited for Gordon: He's far better at confrontation than I am.

"It's nothing," I answered. "Nothing specific. You know how it is . . ."

"Of course, I know." Trent removed my father's bib. "I tell you what. I'm going to head down to the water—just for an hour or so—to take advantage of the light. Why don't you come along with me?"

"I don't know," I said.

"Go on, Abby," Mom insisted. "I can handle your father."

I didn't particularly want to accompany Trent to the shore—not when I knew I'd have to fire him shortly—but somehow I found myself following him down the warped wooden steps between the dune grass. He carried his canvas and tripod under one arm and his supply satchel in the other. It was approaching twilight. A strong breeze blew in off the water, rattling the beach plums. The scent of a distant bonfire carried across the gray sand. "Not many people out here tonight," Trent observed, as he set up his easel. "I guess it's still too cold."

I said nothing. Herring gulls scavenged overhead.

"You've got a wonderful family," said Trent. "Your mother is just a gem."

"Mom has her moments," I conceded.

"She's fascinating. I'm not just saying that. It's hard to believe that I'm talking to a woman who once danced with Mondrian." Trent stepped back from the canvas to assess his work. "I suppose great beauty runs in the family."

"I don't know about that," I answered. "Mondrian was an old man when Mom danced with him. His vision was failing."

Trent's brush waltzed across the canvas. "You're far too pretty to be modest," he said. "And while we're on the subject of modesty, I'm afraid that your older daughter keeps throwing herself at me."

"She does that," I said. "This too shall pass."

"It's quite flattering, you know. But she can't hold a candle to her sister. Did you know that Andromache asked me when I was going to become famous—because she's looking forward to harvesting my obituary." Trent set down his brush and took a swig from his canteen. "That girl thinks about death an awful lot."

"Who *doesn't* think about death a lot?" I snapped.

"Fair enough," agreed Trent. "It *is* horrific, isn't it? I know when my father passed on, I wanted the entire world to stop—to take notice. Even just for a few minutes. But it didn't. The sun still set in the west, and the mail still arrived the next day, and everybody just picked themselves up and went on without him."

"Gordon thinks it's natural," I said. "He's at peace with it."

"He's lucky." Trent retrieved two abandoned wooden lobster traps from the high-water mark and set them up as makeshift benches. He dusted mine off thoroughly. "My mother died when I was fifteen, and I'm still not at peace with it."

"I'm sorry," I said.

I sat down on the lobster crate. Trent returned to painting.

"The part that really gets to me is that she'll never know who I've become. She'll never see my artwork. I'll be ninety years old, and I still won't be at peace with that."

I listened while he recounted his mother's tortuous battle with leukemia, and his father's obsessive hording and self-mutilation. The longer he spoke, the more confident I grew that he'd stolen my jewelry. But I was no longer sure that I wanted to fire him. Maybe a few missing pearls were worth the care he'd been giving my father. I knew that if I told Gordon, my husband would dismiss him on the spot. Instead, I determined to keep one eye on Trent and the other on our valuables.

· · · · ·

From that moment forward, except for the two afternoons each week when Trent was away at art classes, I tried not to let him out of my sight. That meant spending the majority of my free time in the living room, where he tended to my father's health and played card games with my mother. Not that I minded. With the girls away at school and Gordon at the office, I could just as easily write my movie reviews on the escritoire beside the fireplace as anywhere else. Mom was clearly delighted to have the companionship, and Trent didn't object. He appeared to relish having an audience for his grand proclamations on the nature of painting. His own work, as he described it, was "Winslow Homer meets Edward Hopper." I couldn't help reflecting how different this young man was from my husband. If Gordon had ever tried to paint the bay—and I wouldn't have put it past him—he'd have wanted to capture its natural beauty. But for Trent Kendall, aesthetics were beside the point. What interested him was the "devastating emotional power" of the sea. How strolling the desolate shoreline at night forced you to come to terms with your own insignificance. The aide was far too sincere to sound pretentious. Sometimes, he'd speak of the "ebb and flow of lonely tides," and in the very next breath, he'd invite me to play a hand of gin rummy.

While I passed my afternoons with Trent and my parents, I was also careful not to leave anything costly lying around unattended. I locked Gordon's cufflinks and our passports and an envelope full of two dollar bills inside a cast-iron strongbox, and I hid it behind the tablecloths in the linen closet. I removed the silver baby spoons from the display cabinet and tucked them under the lining of my old ice skates. When we emptied out the vaults from my father's shop, I opened a supplementary safe deposit box for the jewelry and coins; the first-edition novels and albums of nineteenth century stamps went directly to my parents' apartment. Short of bolting down the television, I couldn't have made our house any less vulnerable to larceny. Yet Gordon didn't even seem to notice the changes. He was too busy pressuring me to escort him to an architecture convention in Madrid. As though leaving my father alone for a week was a viable option. Besides—although I obviously didn't tell Gordon this—I also feared we might return home to find the house stripped bare to its doorknobs. That's exactly the sort of thing you hear about on the morning news. When it happens to strangers, it's entertaining.

Trent invited me down to the water nearly every evening. My father could no longer keep his eyes open past noon, so he didn't miss us.

"He's losing weight," said Trent.

"I don't understand," I said. "It was a *head* injury."

We were half a mile up the beach, perched on a granite outcropping. Trent's canvas reflected in the tidal pool below. The girls were indoors, watching a rented movie. Gordon was playing tennis at his club.

"It happens," said Trent. "Maybe something about the fall knocked out the appetite centers in his brain. If he were my father, I'd at least consider a feeding tube."

Most of what I knew of feeding tubes related to removing them. That was the controversial, hot-button territory of nightly news broadcasts. But I'd never really contemplated all the suffering that preceded those headlines: That before you took a feeding tube out, you had to put one in.

"Or you could *not* put in a tube," added Trent. "Frankly, it isn't much of a life that man's had these past few weeks. I hate to say this, but he's clearly fading."

"Are you saying I should give up?"

"Believe me, Abigail. I want your father to hang on as much as anybody." Trent smiled affably. "If anything happens to him, I'm out of a job."

"Not as much as anybody," I snapped.

"Of course not," he agreed.

We stood face to face, our shadows long and still.

Trent reached out and squeezed my hand. I didn't stop him. If he'd pulled me to him at that moment, I might have let him kiss me. But instead, he released his grip and returned to his palette. "I don't want to lose the light," he said—too quickly, his voice almost fearful. "You only get so much light, and then it's gone." It was so easy to forget that this was the same man who'd rifled through my purse for my wedding band.

I might have forgotten, too. Except that same night, when I went to lock away a bag of bicentennial quarters that I'd found in the drawer of my nightstand, I discovered that someone had removed the strongbox from the linen closet. It crossed my mind that Gordon might be making off with our valuables, one by one, part of some despicable scheme to salt them away in preparation for a divorce. But that was nonsense, obviously. Wishful thinking. I crossed the foyer in my slippers, took a deep breath and knocked on Trent's door. He didn't answer. I tried the knob. The draught from the open window carried a chill along my bones. The room beyond was empty.

Our home's previous owner, a retired brewing executive, had added the fourth bedroom to lodge a nurse for his autistic granddaughter. It was now a tidy, impeccably arranged chamber whose corkboard-lined walls displayed posters of the Hudson River School masters. Vanderlyn. Durand. Thomas Cole. Works I vaguely recognized from a college "art appreciation" class. The lone bookshelf contained catalogues for galleries and museums, organized alphabetically by nation. A Matisse quotation posted above the nightstand read: *Whoever wishes to devote himself to painting should begin by cutting out his own tongue.* Whatever Trent Kendall's shortcomings, nobody could ever accuse him of dabbling. I might easily have ransacked his belongings in order to recover my own. Instead, I sat down on the narrow, neatly-made twin bed and waited. The young man finally returned after eleven, grinning broadly. I think he might have been drinking. Or possibly, he was just happy.

"Oh, hi," he said. Unfazed to find me in his room. "Is everything okay?"

"Everything is most certainly *not* okay," I retorted.

"How's your hand?" he asked. "Are you fingers still bothering you?"

"My hand is fine," I replied—annoyed that he'd changed the subject. I glanced down at my knuckles. "That was weeks ago."

"I just wondered. Because you've stopped wearing your wedding ring."

Trent pulled his sweater off and slid onto the bed beside me. Close, so I could smell his perspiration and the minty flavor of his breath. It was difficult to think clearly with his face only inches from mine. To my amazement, he took hold of my hand and brought it to his lips. His kisses trailed over my fingertips. I pulled away.

"I need to go," I said. "We'll figure this all out tomorrow."

But tomorrow arrived and I didn't say a word about what had happened. Or about the theft. Neither did he. Our beach conversation—he was teaching me the science behind painting, all about atomic spectra and chromophores and fugitive pigments—picked up right where we had left it. Three days later, I found the iron strongbox in the garage, stuffed into the bin of recyclables.

The clasps had been forced. Our passports remained inside, but Gordon's cufflinks and the currency had vanished. What made me angriest was the missing envelope: How could I possibly be attracted to a man who would steal thirty dollars' worth of two-dollar bills? How could I prefer him to Gordon—who was so patient, so kind, so reasonable? Who was the father of my baby girls! The answer seemed all too obvious: Because I was a terrible human being. Somehow, rather than holding me back, that confession justified everything.

That same week, I caught Calliope topless in her bedroom with a boy from her ballroom dance team. I think I was more embarrassed than she was, but I stood with my arms folded across my chest while she scrambled for her bra. The following morning, my father had a feeding tube implanted at Methodist Hospital. He gained twelve pounds in nine days and was in good enough spirits by the end of May to demand that Trent purchase a handgun. Just in case.

Andromache's bond with the homecare aide intensified. "When you and Daddy die," she asked, "can I go to live with Trent?"

"We're not going to die," I promised her.

"Don't lie to me," she answered. "Grandpa's going to die, and then Grandma's going to die, and then Daddy's going to die, and then you're going to die. That's the natural order of things."

I leaned over her bed and hugged her, silently cursing Gordon.

. . . . .

The irony of Trent's deceit was that, if he had asked, I gladly would have given him the money. We were doing fine financially. More than fine. Even a fifteen-hundred-dollar set of pearls wasn't much when Gordon spent twice that amount each month on private flying lessons. But our employee was far too proud for handouts. He wouldn't even let me reimburse him for Calliope's painting lessons. So I knew that if I accused him of pinching my jewelry, he'd deny it. Then, even if I didn't want to fire him, his own false sense of honor would have compelled him to quit. Far better to catch him in the act—without ever letting Gordon know—and then to force financial help upon him. I told myself I would be doing this on my father's account. Dad couldn't endure another Romanian manhandling. But I suppose my real motive was to keep Trent Kendall living under our roof, because while cheating on Gordon seemed absolutely unthinkable—as outrageous as plunging naked into an icy, fast-moving current—so too did the prospect of Trent falling in love with somebody else.

I fear I may be giving a false impression: Trent Kendall wasn't the only thing I thought about that May, not even after he'd kissed my fingertips. A good portion of my time was taken up in consultation with eldercare attorneys and geriatric psychiatrists, since my father refused to relinquish the management of his affairs. He wanted a court hearing, he insisted. *To show you bastards that I know what's what.* But when I arranged for him to speak with a lawyer of his own, he swore out an affidavit accusing me and Gordon of lacing his food supplements with arsenic. Later, he came down with a fungal infection of his left kidney that spread to his bladder. Calliope also got sick that week: A sporadic case of scarlet fever. While she lay in bed, nursing her headache and fatigue, Andromache planned her sister's funeral—down to the cost of the white lilies and the route of the hearse. She relied on Beth March's illness in *Little Women* to chart Calliope's medical progress. Meanwhile, I continued to watch as Trent painted the harbor at twilight and, when I came down for breakfast one morning to discover Dad's masonic ring missing from his pinkie, I told my mother that I'd removed it. So it wouldn't get lost. By then, my father was once again too incapacitated to care.

That's when I hatched my plot. I'll admit it was nothing particularly ingenious, but it did possess a compelling simplicity. One Sunday morning, before my mother arrived from Creve Coeur, while Dad snored and Trent explained to Andromache how Gilbert Blythe in *Anne of Green Gables* had survived scarlatina, I counted out five twenty-dollar bills and set them conspicuously on the glass coffee table in the living room. I anticipated that when I returned, an hour later, they would be gone. But I also realized—quite suddenly, as I paced that veranda, waiting for Trent to have an opportunity to make off with his loot—that *he* knew that I knew. All along, the goddam thief had been toying with me. He hadn't kissed my fingers because he found me attractive. If he had, obviously he would have tried again. No, all he wanted was to cover his tracks. How stupid could I have been! So when I returned to the living room and found only sixty dollars left on the table, I didn't offer to help pay the man's way through graduate school. Instead, I charged into the kitchen and started screaming at my husband.

"You've got to fire him," I demanded. "I can't take this anymore."

Gordon looked up from the morning paper. He held a cream-cheese-smothered bagel in one hand and a white plastic knife in the other. "Slow down. What's going on?"

"That asshole," I shouted. "Your employee. He stole my wedding band and my pearls and now he's taken forty dollars off the coffee table."

Gordon put down his bagel. "What has gotten into you?" he asked. "*I* took forty dollars off the coffee table. I was going to buy you a Mother's Day present."

"*You* took the forty dollars?"

"I didn't know it was such a big deal," he said. "In any case, you really shouldn't leave money around like that."

I balled my fists together. I didn't want to say anything I'd regret.

"I do hope Trent didn't hear you. We'll never make it to Madrid if he quits on us," said Gordon. He held his index finger to his mouth in order to shush me, then crossed the kitchen and closed the French doors. "Now please sit down and have some breakfast, honey. There's fresh orange juice from the outdoor market."

I slumped into a chair, dumbfounded.

"I think I'm losing it," I said.

"You'll get some food in your stomach," he answered. "Then you'll feel better."

. . . . .

I did not feel better after breakfast. I passed the remainder of the day in bed, listening to the sounds of the house: the drone of air-conditioning, the crescendos of Tommy Dorsey's orchestra, the cacophonic symphony of ringing telephones and flushing toilets and shouting children that made up our life in Midnight Harbor. My mother came upstairs to look in on me around noon. "You take it easy, darling," she urged. "Better an ounce of prevention than a pound of cure." I kept my head facing the wall, so she wouldn't see that I'd been crying. When Gordon brought me a mid-afternoon meal laid out on a tray—chopped pineapple rings, a bowl of chocolate pudding—I pretended to be sleeping. Later, I napped intermittently. It was already well past dinnertime when I finally felt the desire to reenter the waking world. I was overcome by an inexplicably strong yearning to be with Trent Kendall—even to let him kiss my hand again—though I wasn't exactly sure why. Maybe because nothing else made sense any longer.

I stepped into the shower and ran my face under the cool water, escaping into the deluge until my skin puckered. Then I changed outfits half a dozen times until I settled on a corduroy skirt and red cambric top. I didn't dry my hair completely, afraid that sea breeze might ensnarl it. Fortunately, the evening was clear and mild. By the time I arrived at the beach, the sun had dipped beyond the far side of the bay. A pair of bright stars twinkled over the distant pine barrens and, nearer by, tiny waves lapped tenderly at the waterline. Trent sat on an overturned milk crate, folding up the legs of his easel. His canvas rested against a tangle of driftwood.

"I wanted to get in one more day of work," he said matter-of-fact. "The light out here is truly magnificent. I won't get much of that in Newport."

His tone made me uneasy. "How's your painting coming along?" I asked.

Trent snapped the tripod shut and stood up. "I heard what you said."

"What do you mean?"

"I heard what you said this morning. About me stealing things."

"It's all right," I assured him. "I'm sorry I overreacted the way I did. If we were paying you more, none of this would have happened."

Trent glared at me. "The hell it's all right."

"Please, Trent. Be honest with me," I said. "That's all I'm asking. I think I may be falling in love with you, for God's sake. Just tell me the truth and we'll all of put this behind us . . ."

Trent stepped toward me. I thought he was going to engulf me in his arms, but he reached past me for his supply bag.

"You really do think I'm a thief, don't you?" he said.

"Because you are," I shouted. "And I love you anyway. Now swallow some of your fucking pride and trust me."

Trent Kendall shook his head and walked toward the dunes. When he was twenty yards up the beach, he turned back and shouted, in a voice brimming with indignation and disgust, "I've had to swallow a lot of things, Abigail Garrow. But my pride isn't going to be one of them."

He quit that night. Piled his belongings into that weather-beaten Plymouth station wagon, shook my father's quivering hand and presented each of the girls with a newly-minted twenty-dollar bill. Maybe to prove a point. I was still sitting on an overturned milk crate, gazing across the cobalt bay, when I heard a car pull out of the driveway, although it wasn't until later that I learned those headlights had been his.

. . . . .

Gordon didn't ask what had happened between me and Trent Kendall on the beach that evening. He simply accepted the fact that the homecare aide would no longer be working for us. My mother, although she'd genuinely liked Trent, also received his departure with surprising equanimity. "Young men that age aren't reliable," she said unemotionally. "I told you we should have hired an older female. Didn't I say, someone over forty and not too attractive? Though I suppose attractive would have been tolerable, considering how things stand with your father." Dad was even less perturbed. The morning after his bodyguard's departure, he'd entirely forgotten his existence.

It was the girls who took Trent's absence the hardest. Andromache sat at the bay windows every afternoon, waiting for the return of his Plymouth. Calliope wandered the house sullenly, marking her territory with half-empty cans of diet soda. She gathered all of her painting supplies into a large plastic garbage bag and abandoned it at the curbside. If anyone mentioned Trent's name—which did happen, inevitably—she responded with a torrent of profanity. I was so hopeful she might forget about the homecare aide that, when she cut two extra inches off her denim shorts, I didn't have it in me to object. I even let her take boys up to her bedroom and pretended I didn't hear them. But a month later—without warning—she asked if I had Trent's address. It was the Fourth of July. My daughters and I were out on the veranda, waiting for the fireworks show across the bay. Dad was listening to Benny Goodman. Or sleeping. Sometimes it was hard to tell which. Gordon has just left to drive my mother back to Creve Coeur.

"I think it's time to forget about Trent Kendall," I said.

Andromache leaned forward on her chaise-longue and flashed me a look of genuine desperation. "Is Trent really dead?" she asked, "Or is he coming back?"

"No, he's not dead," I answered. "But he's not coming back either."

"Why not?" she persisted.

"Because he took some things that weren't his."

Calliope scowled. "I don't see what *you* have against him."

"I told you, Cally," I said sharply. "He was a thief."

My older daughter made a nasty remark. Not worth repeating. Andromache bolted off the chaise-longue and disappeared into the house. She returned about ten minutes later, carrying a soiled pillow case. She looked as though she'd been crying.

"I also took some things that weren't mine," she said.

She poured the contents of the pillow case onto the patio table. Pearls. Currency. My wedding band. Also costume jewelry, tie clips, silver-plated pens—an assortment of items that I'd never known were missing.

"Jesus Christ," I said. "What the fuck were you thinking?"

I'd never spoken to my children like that. I regretted my tone instantly.

Andromache burst into sobs. "I'm sorry," she cried. "I was just afraid you might die on me and I didn't want to starve."

She stood with her head down, sniveling. Helpless.

"You won't make me go away like Trent, will you?"

I reached into the heap of treasures for my wedding band. "Nobody's making anybody go away," I said gently. "I promise."

"But I'm a bad daughter," said Andromache.

"Come here. Let me hug you," I answered. "Both of you. You're the only daughters I've got."

As I wrapped my arms around my children, children who wouldn't remain children much longer, I understood that I would never again contact Trent Kendall—not to apologize, not for any reason. Already, I was thinking about how to find another caregiver for my father, and about what I would tell Gordon of his daughter's pilfering exploits, and about sticking to the script that life had handed me.

After Valentino

· ·

One summer morning in 1927, a fortnight after the blueberry harvest, Ada Kell bundled herself and her eldest daughter in matching black crepe and set out for the funeral of a young actor neither woman had ever met. Ada's brother-in-law, a livestock agent, drove them to the station in his feed truck. This would have been a two-hour journey, traveling under the best conditions, but three consecutive nights of violent rain had crippled the roadways, churning storm-scarred timber and sheets of corrugated steel into their path. Twice they were compelled to stop—once to roll aside a fallen water tower, and once to assist two elderly sextons reloading a mud-splattered coffin onto a flatbed hearse. *Reminds you of the photos from Europe, from The Marne*, observed George Kell. There's no predicting death nor lightning. Abigail cradled her face in her gloves, weeping for the young actor. Ada wove silent knots through the fringes of her shawl. She'd fought with her husband about taking Abigail to the funeral—he had no use for "picture stars and emperors"—and now she missed him dearly.

Both elder Kells had risen earlier than usual that morning, Ada to pack for the journey to New York, her husband to patch the dislocated slats in the corncrib, but the couple had hardly exchanged a word over breakfast. Samuel Tilden Kell was of a generation that rationed both speech and emotion; he expressed his disapproval like a stone. Although Ada usually relished these moments of muscular reticence—her husband leaning against the cupboards, coarse hair creeping over his neckline, a spool of heavy wire still coiled around his shoulder—this particular morning she'd longed for affection. A dish towel swatting against her rump, even a baritone chorus of "Jeanie with the Light Brown Hair," would have fortified her for the train. All she'd gotten was a soft kiss on the forehead. What made the silence worse was that Ada knew it wouldn't fade when she returned, that she'd married a man who preferred fatal enterprises to foolish ones. But it would pass eventually. Time would work in her favor. If she could bear Abigail's German measles and the baby's scarlet fever, she could endure her husband's silence. Maybe penalties are assessed for everything, thought Ada as they jolted their way across the cratered mudscape. Maybe loneliness is the penalty for love.

George Kell escorted the two women onto the platform with a valise in each arm and a leather satchel tucked under one elbow. He wished his sister-in-law godspeed, repeated his pledge to check in on Samuel, then deserted them to the cigar fumes and detached stares of Albany Station. Several male travelers—two hatless youths, a preacher with an eye patch, an eggplant-shaped salesman carrying a lavender carpetbag—offered the mourners seats in the waiting area. They finally accepted half of a bench from a beet-faced country squire and his gangly son; the squire's wife and three young daughters retained the other half of the bench.

"You've had a loss," said the wife to Ada. "I am very sorry for you."

"Thank you, kindly," answered Ada. "You are most kind."

"And the same week as poor Valentino," chimed the youngest of the daughters. "You have heard about Valentino, haven't you?"

The girl's remark drew a granite stare from the squire's wife and sent Abigail into another spasm of tears. The beet-faced squire offered the girl a handkerchief. The son examined the latticework of cracks in the pavement. The women said nothing further. Ada's best instincts leaned toward correcting the child's error—revealing that they were on route to Valentino's funeral—but she had no desire to salvage the conversation. She had foreseen all of this: The actor's death, her husband's intransigence, the fallen water tower, the mired hearse, George's remark about the Marne, the one-eyed Negro, the girl's mistake, Abigail's tears. And having envisioned much of what had already happened, while also anticipating the better part of what was still to come, Ada preferred to sit in stiff-backed silence, her hands folded across her lap, while waiting for the Albany Mail that would carry them down river to the coast.

· · · · ·

Although Ada suffered twinges of acute clairvoyance, she was not omniscient. Sometimes months or even years might pass without so much as a hint of prophesy. It was almost possible, during these tranquil periods, to forget her powers. Then she'd wake one morning to the clouds of calamity, her fingers tingling, the nerves alive in the roots of her teeth, and she'd see a brief episode of impending pain. Her visions ranged from the life shattering—a brother's bout with cholera during the Spanish War—to the momentarily tender—a daughter's trammeled heart—but they were consistently accurate and uniformly unpleasant. Tidings of marriage and vermilion sunsets always surprised her, more so because she foresaw a future black and grim, because all respite, even the aroma of hyacinth at her father's funeral, was filtered by her prescience. Had Ada been called upon to share these sensations, she might have compared them to the erratic visits of a town crier: It is the voice, more than the words, that conveys the tragedy. But she wasn't called upon and she did not share. Not even with her husband. Silence is the penalty assessed for clairvoyance, Ada thought, because she often knew but could never alter.

Stepping onto the concourse at Pennsylvania Station, her daughter and a porter in tow, Ada experienced yet another of her twinges. An ordinary woman would have seen Ada's older sister, the pharmacist's wife, shuffling across the mezzanine in a brocaded gown, but Ada's eyes pierced both fabric and flesh. As Emmaline approached, one hand holding the knob of her hat, the other fluttering a wave, Ada's arms went prickly and her molars throbbed. She could feel her sister's tumor as though it were swallowing her own liver. Then she saw George driving her and Abigail to the station once again, this time through mid-winter slush, heard the tires of the feed truck grinding over gravel. Ada's first impulse was to flee. She had always, even as a girl, run from death. But flight was impossible. There was no choice but to compose herself—to blot out Emmaline's impending death as she would her sister's dress that reminded her of an upholstered sofa—and to press the dear woman's bony hands between her own.

"Darling Emma," said Ada. "And what lovely brocade."

"This old frock?" answered Emmaline, shrugging.

Ada ran her fingers across the texture. Few opportunities remained to bring her sister joy, maybe an autumn visit if fate and finance permitted, so she treasured the restrained pleasure on the woman's thirsty face. "Abigail," she said, "you ought tell your aunt what you think of her dress."

"Lovely," the girl said mechanically.

"You're both too much, really," said Emmaline. "Now let's make our tracks home and get some hot food into the both of you before you end up as scrawny as I am. The truth is, Ada, I gorge myself, truly I do, but I'm still skin and bones. I've been telling Chester that he should be thankful I thinned out *after* I married him, or I might have taken a better offer."

Emmaline giggled like a sizzling stew and steered her sister across the pavilion. They walked briskly, Abigail and the porter following. Around them swirled the tangled lives of strangers— clerks jostling toward the commuter tram, workmen measuring a grand piano, a teenage girl carrying a potted fern twice her size. At one end of the station an orange-suited warden changed the light bulbs on the chandeliers with a lengthy pike; near the stairway, two palsied women hawked umbrellas and cushions. The crosscurrents of traffic were dizzying, especially to a woman fresh from the countryside.

"I'm so pleased to see you," said Emmaline, confiding, "But I don't understand you.":

"You mean the funeral?"

"Don't you think you're indulging the girl? Next it will be Douglas Fairbanks or William Powell. I'll be putting you up every week."

"It's not only for Abigail," said Ada. "It's also for me. I wanted to see his widow."

"You?" asked Emmaline. "And when was the last time you went to the pictures, Ada Kell? You're spoiling the girl and now you're covering it up."

"I saw her photograph in the paper," said Ada. "She looked so lost, so hopeless."

Emmaline shook her head. "Mark my words," she said. "I'll be putting you up again next summer. But if it takes Rudolf Valentino's dying to see you, so be it. I'm glad you're here."

They stepped onto the curbside and the porter loaded their cab. Ada's molars still ached. She decided against sending her sister to a doctor. What Emmaline didn't know might hurt her, but knowing wouldn't change anything. Fate was fate. The widow Natacha Rambova would ride behind Valentino's body the following morning and Ada would ride behind Emmaline's after Christmas. All one could do was to comfort the living. To hope that they might comfort you.

"Come here, girl," Ada said to her daughter. "No more tears."

Then she wiped Abigail's eyes and embraced her.

·····

At first Ada had diagnosed Abigail's decline as a case of spring melancholy. It's just girlish brooding, she'd told Samuel. As sure as April showers. Her words flowed easily when crocuses poked their tufts through frost, less confident as the pumpkins ripened on the vine. The girl went about her chores without alacrity, moped away her afternoons in bed. She was prone to frequent headaches and sudden fits of sorrow; her features took on the complexion of drink. Ada watched her over the breakfast table each morning, hoping that maternal insight might still succeed where clairvoyance had failed, but Abigail's affliction proved impenetrable. Her deterioration was slow but progressive, stemmed only by weekly forays to the picture show in Chatham. Whatever the source of her pain, the cinema offered a temporary reprieve. The antics of Myrna Loy and Clara Bow—and most of all Valentino—made the pain tolerable. *Maybe a boy*, Ada reassured Samuel. *A heavy heart. The escape does her good.* But when Ada sent her daughter to town more often, first twice a week, then three times, she already knew that she was harming more than helping. The girl's spirits rose with the Indian corn. Valentino's death sent them crashing. Ada examined the haggard child waiting for the cortege of a stranger, her daughter's red eyes sunken in sacks of burlap skin, and she blamed herself for the disaster.

"I shouldn't have sent you to so many pictures," she said.

"I wish I were a starlet, Mama," answered the girl. "Do you know why?"

"Why, darling?"

"That way, if I were to die, you'd be able to watch me again and again.'

The procession saved Ada a reply. Mounted constables advanced in ranks, then limousines festooned with white lilies. Uniformed police officers rode along the running boards. As the formation rounded the corner into full view—black touring sedans as far as the eye could see—restlessness swept the crowd. Hours of waiting under the torrid afternoon sun had subdued the spectators, but also burnt off all vestiges of solemnity, so that it took only the glint of dark glasses behind a windshield and one impassioned shout of Garbo to send them surging. Ada clasped her daughter's hand and the two women reeled forward on their wave.

This time there was no tingling, only pain. Thousands of thin blades slashed across Ada's forearms and wrenched her into the future. Every which way she looked was agony: Clara Bow degenerated into madness; Norma Talmage craving the needle; Jean Harlow, no older than her own Abigail, laid out on a concrete slab. She heard the prison bars slamming on Fatty Arbuckle, felt Ramon Novarro's scalp peeling away under the knife of the mob. Even the majestic Garbo wailed to her from solitude. It was too awful. Then she saw—one final torture after death—the timeworn crypt of Valentino, mossed-over, forgotten, slowly worn to sand. Maybe this is the penalty for living, thought Ada—*but it couldn't be.* She clenched shut her eyes.

She did not open her eyes again until she sensed the crowd dispersing. It might have it been minutes later, or hours. Ada didn't care. Already the procession—the celebrated mourners, the fallen

Adonis, Natacha Rambova in her widow's shroud—were fading down the avenue. She no longer wished to see the widow, to offer her words of comfort. Valentino had not been *Ada's* husband. What could she possibly say? It is enough to bear one's own grief, thought Ada, and the grief of one's children. There was far too much suffering in the world to mourn for others, to comfort all of the living. Maybe the solace of one's own kin was all one had the right to expect.

Ada watched the last of the touring sedans shrinking into nothing.

"Mama!" shouted Abigail, close at hand. "They're leaving."

The girl tugged at Ada's sleeve.

"It's time to go home," said Ada.

"I don't want to go home."

The girl was already running before Ada understood. She had no choice but to follow. It was indecent, two women chasing after a funeral, but much in life was indecent. Was there any decency in ogling a young widow for one's own distraction? Or in a mother passing the curse of clairvoyance down to her child? Maybe the only decent thing left in the entire world was a sobbing young girl on a street bench, hard of breath, searching her mother's face for forgiveness. Or maybe there was hope for the future—yes, indeed, there was—because the mother knew there was nothing to forgive.

"I'm sorry, Mama," said the girl, gasping. "I can't explain."

"It's all right," soothed Ada. "I already know."

She pressed her daughter's head against her bosom. Strangers hurried by, blind, sweating, bent upon their own patch of shade. Ada did not know from whom they were fleeing, from what they were hiding. Their emotional heirlooms were not her concern. Running her fingers through Abigail's hair and along the fragile ridges of her skull, Ada took comfort. Now that they both knew, she reflected, they need no longer suffer in silence. The future might be easier to bear.

"But you don't know, nobody knows," sobbed the girl. "I thought if we got away from home, everything might be different. Fate, I mean. I thought if we ran far enough away, Mama, even the inevitable might change..."

Ada had harbored similar thoughts, but she understood they were fruitless.

"We've run far enough," she answered softly. "And we've suffered enough distractions. Now let us go home and bury your father."

Fallout

· · · · · · · · · · ·

After a long day manufacturing musical sex toys, Maggie's husband studies chemical warfare at the mahogany table in their dining room. He insists his expertise will transfer. Genius is genius. First he gathers up all of his experimental merchandise—panties that sing "God Bless America," clarinet-shaped phalluses that play Benny Goodman's greatest hits—and stashes them under the sink. In their place he stacks volumes with the most menacing of titles: *Tomorrow's Chemical Holocaust*; *An Idiot's Guide to Bioterrorism and Weapons of Mass Destruction*. He's checked out almost an entire section at the branch library and Maggie fears what the librarians must think. She is trying to be patient and giving—that's what pediatric nurses do, after all—but Frank's nightly lectures on paralytic gasses and blistering agents are wearing her down.

The acute fear Maggie senses behind his jittery humor surprises her. It is she—not he—who should be traumatized: *She* was downtown renewing her driver's license when the Trade Center crumbled; *she* was among the refugees who streamed aimlessly over the 59th Street Bridge. He was at his Jersey City office watching CNN. But three days into the tragedy, once they've checked that all of their friends are alive and she's switched her radio from news back to Oldies, when she's thinking that tonight they should try for a baby again, Frank returns from his office lugging three milk crates of books. He smiles with his lips but not his eyes. He says: "I just want to look into some things." She remembers this phrase from his final months of law school, when he brought home the books on starting up a business. He'd read ravenously for several weeks and then predicted: "Well, darling, we're going to be rich." Now he slaps shut the last of his books and announces, with equal assurance: "We're all going to die."

Maggie slides behind her husband's chair and massages his shoulders. She's ordered in pad thai with oysters, even lit a candle in the kitchen. "If that's the way it's going to be," she says, raking her fingertips across his chest and under his tie, "let's die like rabbits."

"I'm being serious," says Frank. He shifts his weight; she removes her hand. "What are you going to do when they start spraying sarin on the subways?"

"Please, Frank," she says. "I've been up since five a.m."

"I know you don't want to hear this," he persists. "But you're going to listen. I love you too much to let you die of anthrax or botulism."

"Nobody's dying of anything," she says.

"Not yet."

Maggie takes hold of his big broad hand and presses his palm against the flesh of her abdomen. This is their code for "Let's go make a baby."

Frank extricates himself. "That's something I've been thinking about too," he says. "Do you really want to bring another life into a world like this one?"

She retreats to the kitchen and packs his untouched meal in foil. He follows her and tries to wrap his arm around her waist, but now she shakes herself free. "*I* want to have a baby," she snaps. "Three weeks ago *we* wanted to have a baby. What's happening, Frank?"

"Maybe it's just something in the air," he says. "I don't know."

When Maggie sees him slumped in a kitchen chair, his shirtsleeves rolled up and his exposed hairy forearms resting on the table, she softens quickly. "Is there anything I can do?"

"It's just something I feel inside me," says Frank. "When I told you five years ago that singing dildos were going to send our kids to college, you believed in me. Have some faith in me now."

"I'm trying. You have to believe me."

"Let's move to the country," he says. "To the middle of nowhere."

She doesn't say anything, at first. She hears the hum of the refrigerator, and at a distance the lonely mewing of the neighbor's cat.

"What's really keeping us in New York?" he asks. "We could go out to the Canadian Rockies. We could do anything. We could start a dairy farm in Vermont."

"We're Jews," says Maggie. "What do we know from dairy farming?"

"That's exactly what my Uncle Mendel said in Grodno. 'We're Jews. What do we know from America?'"

They've been married six years and she still can't keep his relatives straight. "Mendel's the one who tried to assassinate the Czar, right?"

"No," he says. "That's my *cousin*, Little Mendel. My Uncle Mendel's the one who died at Treblinka."

. . . . .

They compromise on three acres in Millbrook Heights. It's a converted carriage house that was once attached to the estate of a Dutch patroon, but the quaint half doors and yellow brick exterior of the seventeenth century structure are complimented by a new wing with an elevated veranda and an indoor Jacuzzi. A three-hundred-year-old oak—once a treaty oak—forms a canopy over the belly of the yard. Financially, of course, the place is a stretch. Maybe even a leap. It also adds another hour to Maggie's commute. Yet the upside is that they're an hour up the Hudson, that they're well beyond what Frank calls *the strike zone*. If Times Square were strafed with napalm, they might not even notice. And there are other advantages too: They will be able to send their children to the public schools and they will be able to grow their own vegetables and they will be able to visit Maggie's father on the weekends. When spring rolls around, they'll even be able to bring the old man home-grown zucchini and patty pan squash.

Maggie's father is serving three years for art fraud: He'd doctored several seascapes purchased at an oyster bar and sold them to a software mogul as Winslow Homers. Since the jury acquitted him of the more serious offense—using the proceeds of the sale to take out a hit on his mistress—he is confined to the minimum-security prison at Wardelsburg. Maggie has taken his side against their mother. She brings him pickles from Riverdale and *maatjes* herring and back copies of *Equestrian Life*. Her younger sister, a librarian on a cruise ship, sends cigars from overseas. Then her sister gets laid off unexpectedly and takes a job as a cocktail waitress. She comes to stay with them until she can get back on her feet. It all happens fast. On their first Sunday in the new house, less than a month after the Trade Center disaster, all three of them drive up to Wardelsburg for the afternoon.

The Wardelsburg prison used to be an antebellum fort; Maggie brings a picnic lunch to eat on the parade ground. She has told her sister several times to dress modestly, but Carreen's idea of modesty permits a bare midriff.

Frank drops the sisters at the gate, but does not follow. There is no love lost between him and Jack Sheldrake: The old man vehemently disapproves of his son-in-law's business ("You have to draw a line somewhere!" he bellows), while Frank calls Sheldrake "Old Fuss 'n Feathers" behind his back. If Maggie or Carreen knew how to drive, he would stay home. When he picks them up at the curbside six hours later, he can't resist a barb. He asks: "Is the Boston Strangler cheating Old Fuss 'n Feathers at poker again?"

"You know it's not that kind of prison," Maggie says. "I told you Daddy rooms with two state senators and a former federal judge."

"The Boston Strangler is dead," says Carreen. "He was stabbed to death in prison."

Frank grins. "Did Old Fuss n' Feathers call the hit on that one too?"

"Knock it off, Frank," says Carreen. "You're playing the wrong crowd."

"Please," begs Maggie. "Let's talk about something else."

They drive silently through the reds and yellows of the valley. Cabins and bungalows speckle the wooded foothills that climb to the horizon. At intervals the foliage breaks to reveal a jaded farmhouse set in a clump of pasture, or a giant plywood apple and an exhortation to "Pick Your Own" at an upcoming exit. There are also goats and stupid-looking cattle. Maggie is relieved they haven't moved this far into the country.

"Different topic," says Carreen suddenly. "How are you two making out in the baby-hatching department? I've been stockpiling names all summer."

Maggie throws Frank a searching glance. He looks about to speak when she says, "We've actually decided to hold off for a bit. Maybe next year."

"That's a change," says Carreen, sounding put out. "I thought you were in quite a hurry."

"With the move and all," says Maggie, sharply, "we've decided to wait."

"These are dangerous times," says Frank. "Quite honestly, we weren't sure if the world was ready for our child yet."

Carreen frowns and bites her lip.

"That reminds me," says Frank. "Take a look in there."

He indicates a large brown paper bag resting on the floor beside the gear shift. Maggie opens it and removes a large rubber face resembling an elephant with an amputated trunk. She looks up puzzled.

"Gas masks," says Frank. "Three of them."

"I thought we were over this," says Maggie.

"Better safe than sorry. I also have CBR suits in the trunk."

"CBR?"

"Chemical biological and radioactive."

Maggie's husband briefly explains that with regular practice, one can learn to don both suit and mask in less than forty-five seconds. His new theory is that the suburbs will be targeted: That's where they can provoke the most fear while facing the least resistance. "And if they do send a crop duster over the property or hit the nuclear reactor at Indian Point, forty-five seconds is about as much time as we'll have. That's why we chose Millbrook Heights. It's the farthest in the area you can get from the reactor and still see the flash. If you're in the meltdown zone but too far away to see the flash, you don't get any warning. Then you're dead."

"Are you for real?" asks Carreen.

"You have to plan ahead," says Frank. "Noah didn't wait for raindrops."

"He's flipped," Carreen says to her sister. "You do realize that, don't you?"

Maggie's eyes implore her sister to keep quiet; Carreen shrugs.

"Tell me, Frank, how far are you going to go with this logic?" Carreen asks. "The next time it clouds over, are you going to build an ark?"

"We don't need an ark," says Frank. "We need a fallout shelter."

. . . . .

Frank finds the architects in the yellow pages. They're a father and son team, J & J Rechter, and while they've never built a fallout shelter—*none* of the fifty-three firms in the phone book has any experience building fallout shelters—they have designed underground firing ranges for several local high schools. Jarvice Rechter's shoulders are broad and stiff like the arms of a coat hanger; he sports a windbreaker and work boots. His son, Jarod, wears a blazer and carries blueprints. Pencil stubs protrude from behind both men's ears.

Since Maggie refuses to expose the architects to the racy merchandise stacked ceiling-high in the living room, their initial meeting takes place on the Feingold's veranda. The visit feels like a social call and Maggie wonders if her sister will hit it off with the junior architect. She serves pink lemonade all around; Carreen tops her own glass off with Tanqueray.

Jarvice Rechter surveys the property. "It's a nice piece of land you have here."

"It's not the country," says Frank. "But what can you do?"

"My second wife had a thing for the country. Not Jarod's Mamma; the one after. She was always on my case to open a bed and breakfast on the coast of Wales."

"She was Welsh," inserts the son.

The father scratches his scalp. "It wasn't for me though," he says. "I sent her out there sure enough and she ended up married to some retired botanist. A Dutchman, I think."

"A Dane," says the son. "From Denmark."

"What I'm trying to say," the father continues, "is that there's city mice and country mice. I'm always going to be a city mouse myself; there's no two ways about it."

A cardboard box under the table catches Maggie's eye. Frank has brought the ridiculous suits and masks out onto the veranda. This is more mortifying than the musical underwear, somehow worse than even the fallout shelter. She quickly picks up the box and carries it into the house. When she returns, carrying an Entenmann's crumb cake and a stack of paper plates, her husband is pacing the deck like an expectant father. Sweat forms a bib on his shirt.

"But you're sure you can do it?" he says. "You're sure your heart will be in it?"

"I'm telling you I can do it," says Jarvice Rechter. "I was merely expressing a personal, non-professional opinion. Speaking man to man, I think you'd be better off building a swimming pool. There's no better exercise than a good dip in the morning. You'll even live longer. Professionally speaking, of course, it's a different matter. There the customer is always right."

Frank nods. "I didn't mean to snap at you, Rechter. It's just that this is important to me. There's a lot at stake." He pours the rainwater off a chaise longue and seats himself on the dry edge. "Anyway, let's do some business."

Carreen takes that cue to stroll off onto the lawn.

Jarvice Rechter strikes a match on his boot and lights a cigarette. "There's lots of ways we can do this," he says. "You want cheap or expensive?"

Maggie's husband does not look at her. She knows she should say something—she envisions a giant concrete shell sucking up their children's college tuition—but thinks it best to wait until later. Frank is much easier to manage in private, she has learned.

Frank says: "We want state of the art."

"It'll take a month."

"Three weeks," says Frank.

"Three weeks," echoes Jarvice. "You pay the overtime."

The two men shake hands. Frank sees them to the door.

Maggie hears the architects' car pull off while she's gathering up the lemonade glasses. She thinks again of Carreen and the junior Rechter and feels her age with sudden intensity: The young architect is the first person she's met who is both a full-fledged adult and conspicuously younger than she. She'd like to share this with her husband, but instead she says: "Do you really think we should give them *carte blanche*? Aren't we strapped as it is?"

Frank examines her as though she's walked off a distant planet. "Sometimes I don't understand you, Margaret," he says. "Why in the world you'd want to bring our protective gear into the kitchen is truly beyond my comprehension. I've must have told you a thousand times: If you don't have it with you at all times, it's a death sentence. You don't want to kill us, do you?"

Maggie is thankful Carreen isn't present to hear this.

"I could barely concentrate after you did that," says Frank. "I kept expecting to see one of those cropdusters shoot by at any moment. Or a flash of bright light beyond the ridge."

Maggie follows Franks's gaze to the ridge, where the hickories and oaks shimmer under the high afternoon sun, almost mocking her with their earthy innocence. Then she does the only thing she knows to do at a moment like this: She shuts her eyes and hugs her husband tight.

. . . . .

That evening Carreen knocks on the door of Maggie's bedroom. Frank has gone out "to think" for the third consecutive night—he drives aimlessly for hours, sneaks cigarettes that stink up the upholstery—so the two women have the house to themselves. Maggie is standing in front of the mirror wearing a thin turquoise camisole when her sister enters; she has also been thinking.

"How do I look?" asks Maggie.

"Like shit. Like you've been crying."

Carreen plops down on the bed and kicks off her heels.

"You know what I mean," Maggie says. "Do you think I'm losing my looks?"

"No. I think Frank's losing his marbles."

Carreen thumbs through a magazine on the bedspread and tosses it onto the carpet. Maggie watches her reflection in the wall mirror. "I'm being serious," says Carreen. "I know you think I overanalyze everything, but this time I'm pretty sure most people would agree with me. What your husband's doing isn't normal."

Maggie isn't so sure. She reflects upon all the times in the past that Frank's weird prognostications have vindicated themselves—from the musical dildos to the warning that her father would end up in the slammer. The world is a dangerous place, after all. She has read a few of Frank's books; even the FBI predicts more terror is likely. Maggie tries to balance these facts against the possibility that her husband is psychologically decompensating. According to her internet research, his symptoms are classic for an obsessive-compulsive display of post-traumatic stress. Of course Frank would never agree to see a therapist. What is there to do but to wait things out?

Maggie forces a smile. "Who is to say what's normal?" she asks.

"I know, I know," says Carreen. "If the Cold War had ended differently, we'd all be dead and those wackos hiding in their bomb shelters in West Virginia would be laughing their asses off. I've heard it all before. You believe what you need to believe. I just couldn't keep my opinion to myself any longer and my opinion is that Frank is in deep, deep trouble."

"Your opinion has been duly noted."

Carreen steps up beside Maggie and preens herself in the mirror. "In any case," she says, "I didn't come by to psychoanalyze Frank." Carreen pauses and takes a deep breath. "I'm leaving."

"It's because of Frank, isn't it?"

"Only partly. It's mostly this suburb thing. Five years on the maritime equivalent of Las Vegas has spoiled me for trees and raccoons and stuff. I want to buy truffles at three in the morning; I want to be surrounded by strangers." Carreen stretches her crow's feet with her fingers. "I'm wrinkling," she says. "I want to meet men."

"What was wrong with boy wonder architect?"

"He's too put together," says Carreen. "I only date shipwrecks. Anyway, it would screw up your chances with this father."

Maggie is caught off-guard. "Jesus, Carreen! He must be fifty."

"And you're married."

"Yes, Carreen," Maggie says sharply. "I'm married."

Maggie throws herself onto the bed. Several of Frank's new products are hiding under the bedspread—feathers that plays "Pop Goes the Weasel" if stimulated—and when the music starts, forming a taunting round, she pulls the toys from under the covers on impulse. She tries to hold her face stiff, but Carreen's laughter is contagious. It takes her several attempts to catch her wind.

"Would you rather be with a man who makes these," she finally asks, holding out the feathers, "or a man who builds fallout shelters?"

"Well, he has a thing for you, just the same. His eyeballs were talking to your thighs all afternoon. And did you notice how many times he emphasized that he was single?"

"How many?"

"Enough." Carreen grins. "You're blushing."

"I'm not blushing," says Maggie.

Maggie catches sight of herself in the mirror; it's not just her face that's turned red, but her neck and the skin above her collarbone. She has given no thought to the architect until this moment. Now she remembers the broad flat swath of his chest. Of course, it's just a passing fancy. She *is* married, after all. *Happily.*

The thought of having an affair is as alien to her as the thought of showing up to work not wearing clothes.

The electronic garage door opens. From below comes the sound of furniture toppling and then a salvo of indiscriminate invective. Frank is home.

"When are you leaving?" Maggie asks.

"Tomorrow. Early."

Maggie rubs her sister affectionately on the shoulder.

Later she takes a long warm shower, during which she thinks about how ridiculous it would be to have an extramarital affair, as ridiculous as her mother refusing her father a divorce, and yet at the same time she is pleased to have considered the idea and dismissed it. The architect's interest is flattering, she admits. But she's not really interested. She'd like to tell Frank how she's decided not to cheat on him, but this is not the sort of intimacy he appreciates. Besides, when she steps out of the shower and drops her damp towel on the bedroom carpet, her husband is fast asleep.

· · · · ·

The various contractors and their building teams appear at daybreak the following morning. Since Maggie works shifts—five days on, three days off—she can sit at the French windows in the library and watch them unloading their vehicles. The variety of conscripts amazes her: surveyors, electricians, day laborers delivered on a flatbed truck. Some of the men lounge on the curbside, sharing cigarettes and copies of the *New York Post*. Others poke about the lawn. The young architect arrives on the scene with a clipboard and is soon engaged in a shouting match with the skeletal, crag-faced Irishman who will manage the excavation. Maggie finds herself engrossed in the spectacle and awed that Frank has launched such an avalanche with merely a phone call.

Around ten o'clock Maggie realizes that nobody's doing anything. A handful of men built like stevedores are tossing around a tennis ball; some of the day laborers are dozing nearby in the grass. The young architect, the Irish excavator and another man are engaged in a heated conference in the driveway. The Irishman periodically vents his frustration by whacking the azalea hedge with a stick. Maggie—more curious than annoyed at the delay— approaches the group with pitcher of orange juice.

"Mrs. Feingold," Jarod Rechter introduces her. "Mr. O'Connor. Mr. DiPenza."

DiPenza is a little grunt of an Italian; he tips the brim of his cap.

"What's all the shouting about?" Maggie asks.

"We're waiting on the building permit," says the young architect. "My father should be here any minute now with the village inspector."

"He gets here," says O'Connor. "I leave."

Jarod smiles benignly at Maggie. "Mr. O'Connor is upset because some of the foundation men aren't union. We'll work it all out."

"Who's upset?" asks O'Connor. "I'm not upset."

DiPenza fingers his mustache. "About that tree . . ."

"Is your husband around?" Jarod asks her. "Or is there a way we can reach him?"

"He's at his office." says Maggie. She's grateful the contractors haven't asked about his line of work. "Is it something I can help you with?"

"It's about a tree," DiPenza says uncomfortably.

"He wants to cut down the oak in back," says Jarod.

Maggie doesn't know how to object. She's always intended to hang a tire from the tree for their children to swing on. "Are you sure you can't save it?" she asks.

DiPenza shakes his head sadly; he appears genuinely grieved.

"Of course you can save it!" The voice belongs to the senior architect; he's approached her from behind with the sallow building inspector in-tow. "Don't you think of chopping down any of Mrs. Feingold's trees, DiPenza."

"The groundwork is going to crack."

"No, it won't," says Jarvice Rechter. "Not if you dig underneath."

The senior architect wishes Maggie a good morning and quickly takes control of the scene. Within minutes the day laborers are back on their truck and gone for good. The stevedores ditch their game of catch; soon they're shouting at each other over the boom of the backhoe. By midday, a well-worn dirt trace curls around the side of the house and the mound of soil in the back yard casts a shadow across the veranda. It is all so well-choreographed: a regular blue-collar ballet.

At first Maggie tries to keep her eyes off the architect. If she gives herself an inch, she fears, she'll take a mile. But fairly soon she gives up all pretense of indifference—she's relocated from the library to the bay window in the living room for a better view— and she tells herself there's nothing wrong with looking. In fact, she finds herself criticizing Rechter's appearance. His brow sticks out; his neck is too thick. An unsightly growth protrudes from one of his cheeks. The architect's own body gives no hint of whether he's forty-five or sixty and she relies upon the son to date the age of the father. She wonders in spite of herself if Carreen is right about his interest.

Jarvice has his opportunities, that's for sure. The workmen make use of the toilet tucked behind the kitchen and if the architect wished to visit the house, he'd have the pretext. Most of the men make several trips inside during the afternoon; she suspects the Irish excavator, O'Connor, has the runs. Rechter never leaves the yard. Maggie watches him down aluminum can after aluminum can of Diet Coke and she senses herself fighting a losing battle against an iron bladder. At some point she sheds all modesty and steps out on the veranda to read a book. The architect waves at her from across the yard and goes back to work.

Maggie is defrosting chopped meat in the kitchen when Rechter taps on the screen door; he's been watching her attempt to separate two frozen hamburger patties with a mallet and chisel. She catches her reflection in the toaster and winces; her white blouse is streaked red. He taps again.

"Do you have a moment?"

"Yes," she stammers. "Sure."

She turns around with her back to the countertop. The chopped meat—maybe because it is Frank's dinner—embarrasses her. She tries to hide it behind her body.

"The work is going fine," says Rechter. "We had to pay those fellows from Ecuador even though we couldn't use them, but that's the cost of business."

"Sure. Don't think twice."

The architect looks around the kitchen. "I'm not here about the work," he says. "Not exactly."

"Oh," says Maggie. She leans farther back against the countertop and feels the perspiration where her palms are resting on the Formica. *If only I'd thought through my rejection speech beforehand,* she thinks.

"I don't know how to say this," says Rechter. "But I'm a pretty straight-shooting guy, so I'll just throw it out there. I want to show you something in the bathroom."

It's less than a second before she knows what he's talking about. Frank's experimental merchandise! Maggie senses the blood leaving her face and she says, "They're my husband's."

"Well the guys have been talking. I just thought you should know."

"It's my husband's business. Oh, Jesus Christ."

Somehow the architect has seated himself backwards on one of the kitchen chairs. "I generally try to keep out of other people's marriages," he says. "But I have a story I thought you might want to hear. Are you interested?"

Maggie says nothing. She clenches her fingers around the mallet.

"Between my first and second wives," he says, "I dated this bank teller from the Bronx. I thought I was going to marry her too. And then one day she takes me to this surprise birthday party for her sister's kid. Streamers, presents—you name it. There's even a cake with twelve candles and the name Isabel carved in icing. Are you with me?"

"Isabel in icing," echoes Maggie.

"There must be two dozen relatives at this thing. We're all hiding behind couches with the lights off and then the sister flicks the switch and the lights go on—and there's no kid. But everybody pretends like there is a kid. You know: Singing happy birthday, making wishes. I swear I thought I was on Candid Camera. Lysette—that's the name of the woman I was dating, Lysette— even starts telling her sister how pretty the girl looks."

"But there wasn't any kid," says Maggie.

"They were humoring the nutty sister," says Rechter. "The kid had been killed six years before in a school bus accident."

Maggie drops the chisel and it clatters to the floor. She prods her brain to sift through the story. "And you think Frank..."

Rechter stands up. "Don't get me wrong," he says. "I'm happy for the work. God knows I need it in this economy. But the other day I couldn't help picking up that you and your husband weren't exactly on the same page with regard to this thing—and speaking completely non-professionally, man to woman, I just thought you should know that I think it's insane."

Maggie feels suddenly defensive. For the first time she's confident that Frank's having some sort of breakdown, but she doesn't want to hear it from a stranger. "Well it makes perfect sense to me," she snaps.

Rechter steps out onto the porch and lights a cigarette. He says through the screen door, "No, it doesn't. It doesn't make sense to you one bit."

· · · · ·

The architect's five o'clock visits become a fixture of Maggie's days off. Although they usually only chat for a few minutes, she pieces together a mental scrapbook of his past. Rechter has served in the Peace Corps, building houses in the Cameroon; that's where he learned he was a city mouse the hard way. He's also been aboard an airliner hijacked to Cuba. Maggie has prepared a long, passionate speech on the sanctity of marriage that she will deliver when he tries to kiss her—but he does nothing of the sort. He keeps the conversation light; after that first day, he never mentions Frank at all. The closest Rechter ever approaches to doing something suggestive is when he returns from the bathroom and says, "I'll be damned. They *do* sing 'Oh Susannah!'"

Progress on the fallout shelter is rapid. The mound of dirt climbs to the height of the catwalk on the carriage house roof and then vanishes one morning on a dump truck; the backhoes give way to a pile driver and a cement mixer. There are a few delays— one of the ventilation men suffers chest pains and is carted away by ambulance—but within two weeks the hulking concrete roof of the fallout shelter appears deep in the bowels of the pit. Maggie cannot fathom the dimensions of the structure. She had pictured a claustrophobic tunnel; this looks more like a summer home underground.

Frank begins ordering supplies: three hundred cans of tomato soup, six fire extinguishers, twenty-five pairs of latex surgical gloves. He's purchased a book called *How To Stock Your Bomb Shelter Without Going Broke* and he follows its instructions to the letter. Yet they are going broke. Maggie manages to carry most of the debt on their credit cards, she dreads what will happen in six months when the mortgage payments come due. It's like building a palace of playing cards and waiting for a wind storm. She expresses her concern to Frank. He tells her not to worry. To prioritize. Who knows if the bank will even be around in six months?

Frank's top priority, it appears, it getting into his CBR suit in under forty-five seconds. He spends most of his free moments on the veranda dressing and undressing to a stopwatch. (The stopwatch, specially designed for the vision impaired, announces the time aloud at five-second intervals. Thirty. Thirty-five. Forty. Maggie finds this countdown ominous.) When Frank pleads with her to practice suiting up, she usually gives in. It is better than watching, listening. Sometimes the two of them spend four or five hours engaged in the futile monotonous drill, and then the stench of treated rubber clings to Maggie's hair for days. Frank manages to reduce his time to thirty-nine seconds. Maggie's remains well over a minute. Whenever she scrambles into the stiff resistant smock, she thinks of Jarvice's ex-girlfriend and the birthday party for the dead girl.

At first Maggie hopes that the fallout shelter will soothe Frank's nerves, but each passing day seems to make matters worse. His "thinking" drives last into the wee hours of the morning and he carelessly burns cigarette holes into the leather upholstery; she fears he may doze off at a rest stop and set himself on fire. Anxiety takes its toll on his appearance: He shaves three times a day and crops his hair short—this facilitates donning the gas mask—but often he forgets to shower and to change his clothes. His eyes sink further into his head; they are permanently bloodshot. She witnesses these symptoms every day, in the parents of children dying from cancer, but this is worse than anything she's ever seen at the hospital. At least in the pediatric wards the children die and the parents tussle on with their lives.

One day Frank asks her to close out their safe-deposit box and to gather together all of their personal valuables—jewelry, heirlooms, their wills—for transportation to the safe in the fallout shelter. Maggie carries the photo albums from their honeymoon onto the deck, where her husband is struggling with the zipper on his protective hood. "Three hundred dollars on these damn things and the zippers stick," he snarls, when he sees her. "Can you remind me to grease them?"

"I'll leave you a note," says Maggie. "In the bag with your lunch."

Frank gives another tug and the zipper pulls shut. "The important thing to keep in mind." he says, "is to put on your suit first and *then* to run for the shelter. It takes over two minutes to make it through the shelter's air seal. If you don't put on your suit and mask *first*, you're dead. Can you remember that?"

"How could I forget?" asks Maggie.

She settles into a lounge chair and opens the photo albums on her lap. The handsome toned playboy staring back at her from the pictures sends a chill up her spine. Here's Frank outside Westminster Abbey; Frank feeding the pigeons in Trafalgar Square. Her favorite is of Frank dodging cars in de Gaulle Circle on his way to the Arc de Triomphe. He'd insisted that was the only way out to the traffic island; she'd snapped the photo and then asked for directions to an underpass. It's hard to imagine the drawn creature cursing at his zipper doing anything so daring. He has the same obstinacy, she thinks, just redirected.

"You have to see these, Frank," she calls out.

"I'm busy."

"Please, dear. For a minute."

Frank lets the sides of the suit fall loose around his waist; the shoulder straps dangle helpless at his knees. He slides onto the lounge chair beside her and vacantly caresses her far shoulder with his hand. "Wow! We were young then," he says.

"Take a look at that," she says. "That's the rent-a-car that got washed away at high tide."

"There was no sign. How was I supposed to know not to park there?"

"There was a sign. It was in Gaelic. Do you remember how scared we were that we were going to have to make good the loss?"

They both laugh.

Every photograph animates another memory; each memory steers them through a long-blocked channel. It's been months— possibly years—since Maggie's had so much fun. She's acutely conscious, of course, that one wrong phrase or glance may break the moment. She prays against all odds that the telephone won't ring, that a delivery truck won't show up on a Saturday. But nothing mars their pleasure. They make it through fourteen albums and eight years of marriage. The sun has fallen behind their treaty oak when she shuts the last volume.

"All done," says Maggie.

She turns to Frank and kisses him; he kisses her back.

"I'm glad you're bringing those into the shelter," Frank says.

"Me too," says Maggie; then she starts sobbing.

"What's wrong?" Frank asks gently.

She shakes her head; the tears won't stop. "I'm so sorry, Frank," she says. "I don't know what to do. Carreen says that we need counseling. She thinks we're both coming unhinged. And I don't know anymore. Can we go together to see someone? Please?"

"Again with your family," says Frank. "Don't pay any attention to Carreen. You're the one who says she overanalyzes everything."

Maggie gropes for her husband and presses her face into his chest. "It's not just Carreen. It's everybody. They all think that you're going crazy." She wants to add, "Even the architects," but something restrains her.

Frank pushes her away and stands up. "Safety isn't governed by democracy," he says. "What people think has no bearing on what's actually going to happen. If they fly a 747 into the nuclear reactor at Indian Point, your sister's vote won't mean squat. Someday you'll see the flash behind that ridge, Margaret, and then you'll thank me."

Maggie cries herself to sleep on the deck; when she wakes up, her limbs are stiff and her clothes are damp with dew.

. . . . .

The following week Frank stops going to work. He can run the show just as well from home, he insists. By cell phone. By fax. He also admits that the commute to Jersey City terrifies him. All those bridges, all those tunnels. "If I'm going to die, I'm going to die," he says, "but I don't want to be buried alive in my car somewhere underneath the Hudson River choking to death on anthrax." Since the fallout shelter is virtually finished—they've covered it over and now it's just a matter of tossing some seeding on the raw patch of earth, also a tweak or two to the electricity and the plumbing— Frank doesn't see the sense of leaving it unnecessarily. "It's a crazy world," he says. "Why take risks?" He sits on the deck from dawn to dusk with his eyes on the skyline.

When Frank refuses to drive her to Wardelsburg to see her father—he'd prefer she didn't go at all; he'll worry himself sick until she returns—Carreen suggests she ask the architect for a ride. This doesn't seem unreasonable anymore. If she's not his lover, she's also not his boss. They've actually become something like friends. At least that's what she tells her sister when at first Carreen begs off joining them. "You have to come," Maggie insists. "I've asked him to bring his son. Otherwise it *will* feel like we're up to no good." When Frank hears that she's got a lift with Rechter, he insists on speaking to the architect directly. Maggie fears the worst. Her husband merely implores Rechter to drive north over the "safer" Bear Mountain Bridge rather than south over the more-traveled Tappan Zee.

Sunday arrives and the Rechters pick up Maggie in their Oldsmobile. She sits up front with Jarvice; they stop by Carreen's place in the city and her sister and Jarod share the back seat. The ride up to the prison is mainly uneventful. Her sister and the younger architect do most of the talking. They both know everything. They become embroiled in a heated dispute as to whether Maine or Minnesota contains the northernmost point in the contiguous United States, and Jarvice is forced to pull over to check the road atlas in the trunk. After that, neither of them says much. At some point Maggie becomes aware that the two of them are holding hands.

All four of them visit Maggie's father. Although this seems like an obvious arrangement (What else would the Rechters do for five hours in Wardelsburg, New York?), Maggie hasn't anticipated the company. Her subconscious has assumed they would vanish and reappear—maybe drive home and back like Frank does. She dreads introducing Jarvice to her father. Jack Sheldrake has a knack for piquing strangers: He compels them to arm wrestle; he tells Holocaust jokes. But the Rechters and the old man get along surprisingly well. They share a good laugh behind the back of the ex-Congressman in the next bunk for whom Jarvice once built two adjacent swimming pools shaped like breasts. Even when Sheldrake congratulates Maggie on finding Rechter—on "trading in the motherfucking pervert" as he repeatedly puts it—the architect laughs off the jest. She suffers only one difficult moment: Jarvice isn't *that* much younger than her father.

The architect drops off both his son and her sister in the city. Then the two of them are alone. They've been alone three afternoons a week for nearly a month, of course, but Maggie is intensely aware that this may be their last moment together. She watches Jarvice, the coarse skin hugging his cheekbones, the sprouts of hair on the backs of his hands. A tired drizzle begins to fall and Jarvice shifts the wipers onto low.

"I got a kick out of your dad," says Jarvice. "He's a riot."

"He can't stand Frank," says Maggie. "That's what you like about him."

"He's fifty-four years old and he's got hormones like a teenager," answers Jarvice. "*That's* what I like about him."

"Did he tell you he's *fifty-four?*" asks Maggie. "He's sixty-seven."

"I figured he was lying. In either case, he's older than I am. You're never going to ask; I know you too well. You're just going to keep wondering, so I might as well tell you. I'll be fifty-two in December."

"I'm thirty-one," says Maggie. "Frank's thirty-six."

Maggie curses herself for saying something so stupid. Why does the architect care how old her husband is? Or—for that matter— how old she is? She thinks of things she might ask him to change the subject: What will his next project be? Does he like being an architect? Each question sounds more asinine than the last.

"Are you afraid of anything?" she asks.

Jarvice chuckles. "Me? Afraid?"

"I'm asking you seriously."

"Growing old," he says. "Growing old and being alone. The usual things. Honestly—and don't take this the wrong way—I'm afraid of growing old and losing it." He switches the windshield wipers off and turns his head toward her. "I don't want to end up like Lysette's sister," he says. "Like your husband. That's my worst fear."

Maggie doesn't have an answer for this.

Outside the leaves are brown and wet. She registers the familiar landmarks—the turnoffs, the crossroads, the house that keeps its Christmas lights up year-round—and she dreads the approach of home. It's is five o'clock on a Sunday afternoon; she should be preparing for a night on the town. Instead they pull up in front of her mailbox. Beyond the thicket of shedding maples, she can make out the lights from the house.

"Here we are," says Jarvice. "Door to door service."

"Thank you. Thank you so much."

"Will I see you again?" asks the architect.

She releases the car door and turns to face him.

"I'm not working for you anymore, Maggie. I have absolutely no good reason to hang around your kitchen. Not. A. *One*." The last three words are barely out of his mouth when she feel his lips press hers, the soft thrill of his tongue against her teeth.

She pulls away, confused.

"You're not offended?" he asks.

She shakes her head. "But I do have to go."

"You know where to find me," he says.

"I'm sorry. I just can't do that."

"I thought it might be this way," he says cheerlessly. "I hope it's alright that I snagged a souvenir to remember you by."

He holds up a small rubber object and squeezes it.

"Oh Susannah!" it sings, "Don't you cry for me..."

. . . . .

The house that Maggie enters feels big and silent. The chandelier in the entryway is dark and the gray light of dusk filters through the long thin windows. Maggie drops her purse on the carpet and leans her back against the front door, the blood pulsing through her temples, her entire body quaking with emotion. She is her mother's daughter, she thinks. Only her mother's daughter could stick to a husband like hers.

"Frank!" she calls. "Frank! I'm home!"

He does not answer.

Maggie wanders aimlessly from room to room, searching for Frank, until she catches sight of him through the living room window. He's out on the lawn. Under the oak. When she approaches him through the twilight, she sees he is carrying several large boxes. He breathes heavily and pauses periodically for rest.

"Jesus, Frank! What are you doing out here?"

"Supplies for the shelter," he says. "I hope you like sardines." He waits for her to wade through the damp grass and says: "I'm so glad you're home. I was afraid something might have happened."

Maggie feels sick, dizzy. "Nothing happened."

"Not this time," says Frank. "Follow me."

He guides her down a steep concrete staircase at the foot of the treaty oak. The steps lead to a narrow tunnel lit by fluorescent panels; the tunnel stops abruptly at a large iron wall. Frank punches an access code into a wall console and an iron gate pulls shut behind them; exactly two minutes elapse (a digital clock embedded in the floor announces the time aloud) and the front door opens into the shelter. Maggie advances into the glaring light.

"Here we are," says Frank. "What do you think?"

The room resembles a low-budget efficiency apartment. Assorted boxes are stacked from floor to ceiling along three of the walls, also across the countertop in the kitchenette. The fourth wall is composed of exposed cinderblock. Some loose items are also stacked haphazardly on the office carpeting: sacks of brown rice, coat hangers, cartons of baking soda. Frank leads her through the complex and she notes that one of the rooms contains a bed and another a billiard table; they are otherwise equally cluttered and equally indistinguishable. The air smells pungently of mildew. Maggie's first thought is that Jarvice has constructed all this; she tries to be impressed.

"It's pretty amazing," Frank says, beaming. "If it proved necessary, we could live down here for six weeks. Maybe eight."

"Eight weeks," echoes Maggie.

"That's how long the generators run without recharging."

"Oh," says Maggie.

Frank seems so calm; he's more relaxed than she's seen him in weeks.

"Let's get some more boxes," says her husband.

They return to the lawn. The boxes earmarked for transport are lined up along the floor of the veranda and Frank slides one of them out of the way with his foot. Maggie notices the bottoms of some of the cartons are soggy with water. Frank stoops over to pick up what looks like a case of bottled beverages—when his back stiffens and his entire head jolts back.

He shouts: "A flash on the ridge! A flash on the ridge!"

Maggie turns to see several bursts of light on the horizon. They are softer than she has been led to expect—more like trucks driving off the interstate than a nuclear meltdown—and the stopwatch has announced the passage of ten seconds before she starts putting on her suit. She pokes her arms through the smock, slides her feet through the legs. The timer speaks: "…Twenty-five…Thirty…" She finally tucks everything in place when the zipper jams on the hood.

"Goddammit!" she shouts. "It's stuck!"

"I told you to practice!" shouts Frank.

"…Thirty-five…Forty…"

Frank is already fully garbed. He swats her arms away and takes hold of the zipper; when he tugs, it pulls shut around her mask. She is safe.

"…Forty-five…"

"Hurry up," says Frank. "Follow me."

Maggie doesn't move. Frank's confident smile rapidly fades to wonder and then terror; he starts shouting at her, but she can't make out the words. It is like watching someone on the other side of the glass walls of an aquarium. Her husband is shouting, waving his gloved arms. He attempts to grab hold of her, but she dodges his fingers. She wonders how long he will wait before abandoning her on the deck.

There is a soft glow over the ridge: It is either a nuclear meltdown or a freeway fire or something entirely unforeseen and inexplicable. And somewhere out there is a woman throwing birthday parties for a dead child. And somewhere else out there is her father and her sister and Jarvice Rechter, especially Jarvice Rechter.

"…Fifty…Fifty-five…"

She throws open the mask and breathes deep.

Jacob M. Appel is a physician, attorney and bioethicist based in New York City. He is the author of more than two hundred published short stories and is a past winner of the Boston Review Short Fiction Competition, the William Faulkner-William Wisdom Award for the Short Story, the Dana Award, the Arts & Letters Prize for Fiction, the *North American Review*'s Kurt Vonnegut Prize, the *Missouri Review*'s Editor's Prize, the *Sycamore Review*'s Wabash Prize, the *Briar Cliff Review*'s Short Fiction Prize, the H. E. Francis Prize, the New Millennium Writings Fiction Award in four different years, an Elizabeth George Fellowship and a Sherwood Anderson Foundation Writers Grant. His stories have been short-listed for the O. Henry Award, *Best American Short Stories, Best American Nonrequired Reading, Best American Mystery Stories,* and the Pushcart Prize anthology on numerous occasions. His first novel, *The Man Who Wouldn't Stand Up,* won the Dundee International Book Prize in 2012. Jacob holds graduate degrees from Brown University, Columbia University's College of Physicians and Surgeons, Harvard Law School, New York University's MFA program in fiction and Albany Medical College's Alden March Institute of Bioethics. He taught for many years at Brown University and currently teaches at the Gotham Writers' Workshop and the Mount Sinai School of Medicine.